Nightcrawlers

Alexis Bonn

Published by Trellis Publishing, 2021.

This is a work of fiction. Similarities to real people, places, or events are entirely coincidental.

NIGHTCRAWLERS

First edition. June 30, 2021.

ISBN: 979-8224791668

Written by Alexis Bonn.

NIGHTCRAWLERS

ALEXIS BONN

As she was about to close her email for the night and go to sleep, Sara heard that familiar little beep. A new message was waiting for her. It was an email sent through her YouTube account, which she had filtered as soon as her channel had taken off. It was only 9 months ago that she started uploading videos of her adventures but she had really started ghost hunting years earlier. As a kid, she and her brother would dare each other to go into the creepy abandoned houses on the other side of town. They fascinated her with their old architecture and their decrepit walls. She couldn't believe that houses that looked so lifeless, used to be alive with the sounds of families. Somehow, they never scared her, though she pretended to be for her brother.

She truly loved exploring them. What she loved even more was the attention she got from telling her friends about her brave trips inside. She never had enough of that. From the age of 8 and all the way through high school, she regaled anyone who would listen of dark stories filled with supernatural events that she made up off the cuff. Not everyone believed her but it was hard to deny how good of a story teller she was.

And as a new college graduate from a media arts school, she had dedicated her first year of adulthood into creating this persona of an extreme ghost hunter. Her success was overwhelming, even to her, and her fame seemed to grow exponentially every day. She was now even recognized on the street and asked for autographs. That, of course, made all of her sleepless nights and uncomfortable overnight stays in creepy old houses worth it.

The email was still bold as she clicked on it. It was an invitation to fly across the country to Louisiana sent from "The Conservation Collective of Pre-Civil War Phantasmal Plantations". She read it carefully.

Dear Ms. Sara Elliot,

The Conservation Collective of Pre-Civil War Phantasmal Plantations would like to extend an invitation for you and your crew to spend a night in one of our oldest and most spectral houses. It is called "The Lynch Plantation" named after its original owner, although its name holds appropriately with its history. Mr. Lynch was said to be the cruelest man in the south and lynched all of his slaves when he found out that the war had been won by the north. Surprisingly though, his story is not the one that the locals remember. Called Pi Beta Die by the locals, this house's last use was to house a sorority for the local university. 15 years ago, the maintenance man assigned to the house had a psychotic break and killed all 24 members of the sorority then hung himself on the porch outside.

It is our belief that the Lynch Plantation's history is enough to interest you but to further encourage you to create an episode for this house, we have arranged all of your travel and accommodations. You will see the details in the attached document.

The Conservation Collective of Pre-Civil War Phantasmal Plantations seeks to get more publicity and therefore more funding for our cause so please send your reply as soon as possible.

Best Wishes,

The CCPCWPP

She was hooked. Instead of going to bed as planned, she stayed up all night reading and researching the sordid history of the plantation. It was even more incredible, terrifying and mysterious than they had let on in the email. She knew that a night in this house would solidify her as YouTube's leading Ghost Hunter and may even lead to her getting her own show. She knew her fans well. They would love the creepy historical aspect and eat up the sorority massacre with a spoon. When she was too excited to wait, she dialed the number of her main camera tech Lila.

"Its 6:45am Sara, you better have actually seen a ghost," she grumbled. Lila wasn't a morning person and she had known Sara for long enough to know that most of her "ghost sightings" were fake and in fact was one of the people responsible for how real their "encounters" looked.

"Lila, if you wake up now and listen, I'll buy you Starbucks and give you a raise," Sara said. She knew Lila couldn't resist coffee.

"What is it?" she asked, sighing.

Sara beamed with enthusiasm. She knew that it was coming across through the phone because as she explained the email, Lila became more and more alert and excited.

"This could be huge for us Sara!"

"So you're in?" Sara said, knowing that she didn't even need to ask. "Duh!"

"Ok ,we have to get the guys to agree too." Sara coached.

"Just promise them an adventure and to keep them when you get your own show," Lila said nonchalantly. Of course the rest of the crew would agree. The guys were in their mid-twenties and could be pacified with a cheeseburger.

The next few days were filled with preparation. Sara responded to the email to agree to the trip and outlined what she needed when they arrive and explained who she was bringing. The impression she got from the responses were that the more the merrier. Finally, they were all on a plane from Washington to Louisiana. The guys slept the whole way, snoring loudly of course. Sara and Lila sat together to write the script for the background and opening. They would shoot the outside of the plantation and house during the day and have shots of Sara explaining all the details she found about the mass lynching and murders.

By time they arrived, Sara and Lila had all of their shots planned and a script all laid out. Even though they were itching to go straight to the old house, The Conservation Collective of Pre-Civil War Phantasmal Plantations contact insisted they check into a hotel and get settled and rested. They would begin their investigation and shooting tomorrow. They were all smiles and splurged on room service and watched TV on the flat screen. The hotel was obviously very old but well-kept and the rooms were modernized for the guests' comfort. The lobby was small but elegant with two rows of white pillars that led out to the street. After they were stuffed, they decided they needed to walk it off by exploring the bustling town around them.

It was a warm October night so they skipped their jackets and made their way down the old fashioned road. The buildings were tall and thin and the antique street lights cast long shadows against them which no one else seemed to notice. The group weaved their way in and out of the busy streets watching the locals as they enjoyed the many bars and cafes. Andrew, one of the sound techs was mesmerized by the voodoo shops he saw and dragged Colin, another camera guy, in with him. He bought them all incense and they laughed as they all wandered the streets with the potent twigs. Finally they settled on a quiet smoky café. Knowing they had to be awake and alert the next day, they all opted for coffee or tea. As they sipped the delicious, hot beverages, they began to discuss the plan for the next day.

"Ok, I think we should be all packed by 11am. I want to make sure we can get to the location and have plenty of time to explore the plantation before sunset. We also need time to shoot the outside shots with the narrative and set up camp inside for the night," Sara said.

"I agree," Lila said. "Colin, I know you have that 4k camera that can work in low light. Hoorah for that. I was thinking we'll start outside and work our way in. We'll shoot like we always do, start in the living room, I'll explain the history of the house then we'll pretend we'll hear something and head upstairs."

"You want me to add a sound effect in post?" Colin asked.

"Yeah, of course," Lila said. "As long as its not too cheesy. Has to sound real. Like a ghost screaming or something."

"I have no idea what that would sound like," Colin laughed.

Lila covered her mouth and made a groaning sound. "Like that."

"Sounds like a bullfrog with indigestion."

Well, you know what I mean. We'll worry about all that later."

"Done deal."

"Of course, we will have to wait until we see it in person to make the final decisions but Sara and I have pretty much memorized the property maps and house floorplans." Lila finished.

"How creepy is it that it's called "Lynch"?" Andrew said.

Matt, their back-end video editor, chewed on some cookies as Andrew glanced his way.

"What? Just cuz I'm black you look at me?" Matt said jokingly. Andrew gave him a little, playful shove and they laughed.

"I'm just saying..." Andrew said with a laugh, "If there is some sort of evil ghost there... you might be the first to go."

Colin nudged Matt, "Don't worry man, I got your back!" Then they all started laughing.

Sara really enjoyed her crew. They were as silly as they were serious and worked as hard as she did. But they also brought her out of her head and gave her time to be sarcastic and have fun. She smiled at them. Then she saw a young woman lean over to Andrew.

"Excuse me... Uh... were you talking about going to the Lynch Plantation?" she asked, looking more than a little concerned.

Andrew grinned, apparently not picking up on her trepidation. "Yep! First thing tomorrow!"

The blood drained from her face. "Why... why would you go there?" she asked, her voice shaking.

"See that girl over there?" Andrew pointed to Sara. The girl nodded and Sara gave a little wave. "Well she is a ghost hunter and also a tiny dictator. We go where she tells us," he said sarcastically. A tone this young woman missed.

She looked directly at Sara. "You need to stay away from there."

Sara laughed nervously. "Oh come on... It's just a house. We will be there one night and that will be it."

The young woman looked even more terrified. "You're staying the night?!" she asked. Her voice carried enough that the rest of the people in the café turned to look at them. The soft music in the background stopped playing.

Sara and her team suddenly were the center of attention. Something that Sara was only comfortable with when it was filmed, not live. She looked at all the faces staring back at her. "Yea... that was part of the contract. My team and I have been paid to make a show for it... to raise money to restore it. It will bring more tourism to this town."

"Restore it?" the young woman asked. "We don't want it restored and we certainly don't want any tourists coming here only to be killed by going in that house."

The other patrons in the place nodded their heads in agreement.

"Listen, I have been all over the United States. I have stayed in over a hundred haunted houses. Nothing violent has ever happened and no one has ever been hurt." Sara said, choosing her words wisely. She wanted to tell them that all of this ghost business was crazy and that she had never encountered anything supernatural, but she didn't want that to get out and damage her show's credibility.

"All due respect... you've never stayed in this house." Another guy said from the corner. Sara's crew looked around at the petrified faces.

"So none of you ever go there? Even out of curiosity?" Colin asked.

"The last person that went there out of curiosity was found hanging from the porch the next day." The young woman replied.

"Maybe he was depressed and chose to off himself there." Andrew suggested while rolling his eyes. If anyone was a skeptic, it was him.

"He was my brother," she said. Andrew looked mortified and wished his tea had a shot of whiskey in it.

"Oops," he muttered, wishing he could say more.

"I'm sorry for your loss but we were paid to do something and we never back out of a contract." Sara said while Andrew stared at the table in front of him. "Now, I think we should be going." She said as they all stood up.

They shuffled out of the café and began walking towards the hotel quietly. They were all silently trying to brush off the many warnings they had just heard and get their excitement back.

"It's ok guys, some places just really buy into this crap." Lila offered.

"Yeah... but we have never had that reaction from any other location," Matt said. "Those folks are serious about this shit."

"Come on guys," Sara said. "This is a beautiful, creepy, historic building. It's going to be great, AND safe." They were probably just hazing the out of towners. I bet they're probably in there right now laughing their asses off at scaring us. Well, we'll let them think that way."

"Hey, uh... excuse me! Wait!" They heard someone say behind them. They turned. It was another young woman who had been listening silently in the café. She ran up to them and stopped. "Sorry, its just... we were wondering... who paid you to come here?"

"Um, it's a group called The Conservation Collective of Pre-Civil War Phantasmal Plantations. I believe they support and restore these kinds of places all over the south and have a lot in this area. I looked them up, their headquarters is just on the other side of town next to a Piggly Wiggly on 2nd street." Sara replied.

The girl looked around at the group with a strange expression. "That part of town has been completely abandoned for 10 years. There was a hurricane that destroyed it and we didn't have enough money to restore it... and as far as I know, there has never been a group by that name in this area. And I have lived her my whole life. I really don't think you should go to the plantation... someone is setting you up."

Sara looked uneasy but Andrew stepped forward.

"Listen, we appreciate your concern but I am sure there is a reasonable explanation. No one would spend this much money on a prank. Now tell all your buddies at the café that we aren't backing down."

Sara looked at the girl. If anyone had spoken to her like that she would have just let them walk straight into a moving car. But this girl stood there with panic on her face. She knew she couldn't say more but still looked like she wanted to stop them somehow. Her facial expression gave Sara goosebumps but before she could even consider breaking the contract, Andrew and Colin started leading her toward the hotel.

"This town is full of crazies." Matt said under his breath.

CHAPTER TWO

Sara didn't sleep well that night. The scene in the café played in her head over and over. She lay awake listening to everyone else snoring. Finally, she flopped over to look at the clock. It was 3:19 am. She groaned quietly. She thought about how excited she had been for this and managed to talk herself back into the adventure before her, deciding that the townies just didn't get out much and had possibly seen too many movies. She fell asleep.

By 11am exactly, their van was packed and any trace of hesitation from the night before was gone and the silliness had returned. Colin was shooting footage of their drive on his phone. Sara and Lila were taking selfies with all of the equipment. Andrew was driving, as always and Matt was snoozing in the front seat.

After a 40 minute drive, passing through the town, driving past the university, they finally pulled up to a large flat expanse. There was a dirt road jetting off to the left and a large sign above it that was covered in dust. Matt jumped out and managed to jump up to wipe the dust away. Sure enough it said "LYNCH". Colin couldn't help it, and he jumped out to take a picture of Matt standing under the sign with both hands flipping him off and a huge grin. They all giggled and rolled their eyes. Then they took off down the dusty dirt road. The large house grew as they neared it.

"I knew it was a mansion but I guess I didn't think it would be this big." Lila said.

"What do you think a sorority was thinking in buying something like this?" Sara asked.

"Simple, they could have keggers and ragers without the neighbors complaining." Colin said. He was the only one who had been a part of Greek life. A part of his past he tried to suppress.

They pulled up to the front of the house and climbed out. For a moment they just stood, appreciating its old fashion beauty and its size. It was gigantic. The wrap around porch alone was bigger than Sara's apartment. Sara and Matt continued to look over the house and the land while Lila, Colin and Andrew unpacked the equipment. When they finished, Lila walked up to Sara to make a game plan.

"It's hard to believe that the townspeople wouldn't want to save this place. It's so beautiful." Sara whispered.

"I know. Like look over there! Past that field it looks like there is a pond and small wooded area. And this tree over here would be great for a giant swing..." Lila said as she approached an old Oak tree that was closest to the house.

"Its really big. Like really big. This is going to be our best shoot yet," Sara said.

"Where should we start?" Lila asked.

Sara looked around thoughtfully. "Ummm... let's begin with the civil war history of the plantation and slaves with the fields in the background. Then I will walk to the tree and end at the porch when I talk about the sorority massacre. Got it?"

Lila nodded once and set up her camera. She began rolling as Sara started to talk.

"Hello, today we are in Louisiana at their best kept secret haunted destination. The Lynch Plantation is over 200 years old and has a most interesting history. Built by a Slave trader and his wife in the early 1800s, this plantation was one of the largest and most profitable in the area. Although aptly named for the fate of over 300 slaves, the Lynch plantation actually received its name from the slave trader who built it. James and Mary Lynch became exceedingly wealthy from the cotton cultivated here. Once the war was won by the north, they knew that their way of life would never be the same. Already know to be a cruel master, James Lynch decided that his final act of rebellion against the north was to kill all of the slaves he held. Most of them were hung from the branches of this oak tree but the younger children and smaller women were drown in the pond at the back of the property.

Then the bodies were collected, placed in a pile and burned at the entrance where you can still see bits of burn marks today. Only 5 years after the mass lynching, Mary Lynch suffered a psychotic break, claiming that the ghosts of those she helped kill were haunting her. She stabbed her husband and then hung herself on the porch right here. But perhaps the most famous suicide on this porch was that of mass murderer Gary Lindale. Gary, a maintenance man from the university was hired specifically to look after the needs of this house while it served as the Pi Theta Kai sorority house. He lived in a small servant house that used to stand just over there but has since been demolished. One night, Lindale snapped, much like Mary Lynch and went on a murdering spree killing every single sorority girl inside. He then called 911, left the phone off the hook and hung himself in the exact same place as Mary.

This house certainly is one of our more chilling explorations and we invite you to join us for a night at the Lynch Plantation." Sara said and stopped. That was the cue for Lila to stop rolling. It never ceased to amaze her that Sara could do these on the first take with no notes in front of her. She was a natural.

"Let's say we explore, take pictures and maybe some landscape footage?" Sara asked Lila and Colin.

Andrew and Matt were right behind, having a heated debate about which sorority girls they thought were the best partiers. Sara and Lila tuned them out, focusing on the expanse in front of them. The sun beat down and even in mid-October, the heat made them sweat. For a moment, Sara imagined what it would have been like to harvest in this heat as a slave. She let herself mourn the loss of the hundreds of innocent lives. She didn't believe in the afterlife so she hoped that death was a welcomed rest for them. They explored until the sun got low in the sky.

"Guys we should go inside and set up now." Matt said, turning to the house. They picked up the equipment from the ground outside and walked up the creaking steps to the front door. Lila pulled out a small camera and filmed Sara as she turned the doorknob and pushed. The door gave way with a small squeak. They slowly made their way inside. The entry way was covered in dust but other than that, it looked as though the owners had just stepped out for a moment. There was furniture set up as if company was expected. The long dining room table was set as though the sorority girls were going to sit down to dinner together. They made their way down the hall and through each room. Colin and Lila were shooting footage of everything. Finally they made their way to the living room. It was beautifully decorated and the fireplace even had logs in it ready to be lit.

"Matt and I will set up the cameras in the rooms and upstairs. Lila, you and Colin make sure that the feeds are working and tell us about positioning." Andrew ordered. He was excited. While the rest were busy with their tasks. Sara decided to watch the footage they had gotten before including her intro. She sat on the dusty old sofa and turned on the camera. The footage was even better than she had hoped and for a moment, she was extremely grateful that she had found such talent in Lila. As the video wrapped up she saw the frame of the entire house. Once more she took in the beauty until she noticed something. She paused the video and zoomed in. Up on the second floor in one of the bedroom windows stood a woman in a very old dress staring directly into the camera.

Sara took in a huge gasp of air and blinked. She looked again and the figure remained. She waved her hand toward Lila.

"What is it Sara?" She asked seeing Sara's horrified face.

"Colin, can you see me? How is this?" They heard from the microphone attached to the camera that Andrew was placing.

Lila moved over and looked at what Sara was pointing at. They replayed that part of the video and they were both speechless. They continued to watch through to the end and that was when they saw something even more startling. As Sara had approached the porch and was explaining Mary's hanging, the woman disappeared from the window and suddenly appeared right behind Sara holding a noose. They both gasped in fear.

"That's good Andrew, I think that's the best shot." Colin said into the walkie talkie.

Sara and Lila looked up to see the screen that Colin was watching. The video feed was of Andrew in the same room that the woman had been in in the video. "Andrew!" They both shrieked. Colin jumped in surprise.

"What?!" Andrew said from right behind them. They jumped and turned to him.

"How... you were just..." Sara stuttered.

"There is a 30 second delay. Geez what's wrong with you two?" He asked. They showed him the video while Colin helped Matt navigate setting up a camera in another room on the second story.

Andrew was just as stunned as they were. "I was just in there and there was nothing weird..." He said trying to talk himself down.

Then Lila got an idea. "Colin play back the footage you have of Andrew setting up the camera." She said.

"What..? Why?" He asked confused. He had been too distracted to hear their conversation.

"Just do it." Sara screeched. He did and they saw the room in night vision. It glowed in a soft green and they saw Andrew fumbling with the equipment.

"How long have you been doing this for now Andrew?" Colin teased but no one laughed.

Then just as Andrew leaned over to place the camera and backed away they saw her. The woman was right behind him holding a noose. Colin, who hadn't heard anything before that jumped back and screamed. "What the F***?!" They watched Andrew leave the room and the woman with the noose remained staring into the camera, unmoving. Then finally she turned her head and seemed to float out of the room.

They sat watching the camera in silence until the walkie talkie beeped, startling all of them.

"Colin, Colin! Is this ok? I don't want to be up here alone any longer. It gives me the creeps!" Matt said.

Colin immediately switched the video feed to Matt's camera only to see a close up of his face.

Sara held her breath. She wondered if the woman would appear in that room too. She grabbed the walkie talkie.

"Matt... uh... can you back up so we can see the room." She said with her voice shaking. They watched for 30 seconds and then saw him nod at the camera and back away. Just as they got a glimpse of the room, the feed cut and they heard a thud.

"Matt!" Sara screamed. They watched the screen and saw that it was flashing between black and night vison. When it stopped flashing, it showed something that drained Sara's blood. It was the woman holding the noose and standing next to a tall man in the same period clothing. And at the bottom of the screen they could see Matt's still body.

Andrew and Colin jumped up and ran to the staircase. Lila and Sara could hear their heavy footsteps above them. Lila stared at the screen with a strange expression on her face.

"Wait... that man... I've... I've seen him before. She reached for her laptop and opened it to a bookmarked page. It was an article from a newspaper covering the massacre of the sorority sisters. There were pictures of all 24 victims and a picture of the man who killed them. It was the same man.

Sara and Lila looked at both images in utter confusion. Then the feed from the room was cut completely and just as suddenly, the power went out. The darkness surrounded them and they screamed. In the corner of the room, a giant clock struck the hour. It was only 10 pm but it felt so much later. After the last chime, the power came back on and everything was quiet. Lila and Sara first checked to make sure the other was ok then looked around them. But when they looked at the walls, both felt as though the wind had been knocked out of them. All of the paintings, pictures and decorations were upside down.

They bolted up and ran to the stairway. As they climbed they saw the upside down portraits smiling sadistically at them. That's when Lila first saw it. Blood splatter on the wall. It looked fresh.

"Andrew! Colin! Matt!!??" She screamed and they ran up the stairs.

"Down here." Andrew's calm voice beckoned them to the last room on the right. Matt was sitting on the floor and Andrew was standing next to him. Colin was fiddling with the camera.

"I just told him what we saw." Andrew explained. "He doesn't believe me." Matt was clutching his head.

"What happened? Did they get you?" Sara asked breathlessly.

"Not you too... listen guys this isn't funny ok? My head hurts from knocking it on that shelf and I am not in the mood for a practical joke." Sara was about to try to reassure him that it was no joke when they heard the door behind them creak.

They turned to see a beautiful blond girl standing in the doorway. Her hair was disheveled and there was blood dripping from the side of her mouth and oozing from her sides and arms. "He's coming. You'd better run... although it never helped any of us." She said as her cold blue eyes looked past them to the window.

Then the lights went out again and flashed back on. She was gone and all that remained was a bloody hand print on the door frame.

"Believe me now?" Andrew said. Sara had no idea how he could care about that at a time like this.

"We need to leave." Sara said rushing to the door. But as she ran into the hall, she saw the same man as before wearing modern clothes and wielding a large knife. She saw blood splatter l lining the walls. He was blocking their way to the stairs. She looked around at the other bedroom doors that were slightly ajar. None of them would protect them. Then she looked up. There was a rope that pulled down a ladder to the attic.

"You guys!" She said as she yanked it. The man at the end of the hall started walking slowly towards her, undeterred by her possible escape. They all scrambled up the ladder and slammed the entry way shut before the man with the knife could reach them. They heard nothing. They sat in the dusty attic and silently tried to think of how to escape from the top floor of a mansion without going back into it. Though they were not really safer than before, the attic gave them a false sense of security and they all tried to breathe. Lila looked over at a box near them. She pulled out a very old painting. Though it was dark, she could make out that it was a couple. She pulled out her phone and used the light to look at the image. When she saw it clearly, she nearly dropped it.

It was the same man and woman they had seen in the video. But not only that, the man was identical to the mass murderer who killed the sorority girls 15 years prior. She read the bottom of the frame, "Mr. and Mrs. Lynch".

"Guys..." She said and showed the picture to the others.

"So what was this guy reincarnated or whatever?" Andrew asked. It was strange to hear that from a skeptic.

Just then, the ladder to the attic began to shake. They all looked around to find a way out. There was a tiny window at the other end of the attic. They ran over and Colin broke the old glass with his foot. Sara slid out first and they lowered her on to a part of the roof over the second story. Then it was Lila's turn. When they were both out, they crawled along the shingles to find a place they could climb down to the ground. They found nothing. By time the guys had slipped out, they had found the only possible way off the roof was to lower down into one of the bedroom windows. Andrew went first to break the window and help grab the others. Lila went first, then Colin. When it was Sara's turn she briefly looked around the property and the dirt road. The moon was much brighter than she thought it was and it lit the whole plantation. That was how she saw him. There standing against an old truck was a man, just watching the house and watching them climbing in. He didn't move.

"Do you see that man?" She asked Matt. He looked to where she was pointing and shivered. Something about the man by the truck gave him a sickening feeling.

"Yea... but we can't worry about him right now. We have to get out of here." Matt said.

He helped her lower down then quickly climbed down himself. They all made their way to the door and into the hall. Just as soon as they had stepped into the hall, the man reappeared with his bloody knife.

"Into the rooms!" Andrew screamed and they split up into each room.

They slammed the doors and turned the latches, each praying that the doors would hold from the phantom killer. But no sooner had they each locked the doors when a chorus of screams sounded. Hearing this, Sara turned around to face the room she was in. There was blood everywhere. The walls were covered and there on the bed was the body of a dead girl who had been stabbed over 10 times. Sara let out a cry. She heard the same sound come from Lila in the room next to her. They were all seeing the crime scenes of the girl that had died in each room.

Tears rolled down Sara's face. She ran to the window to try to open it. She would jump if she had to. A broken leg was better than dying. But it wouldn't budge.

"It won't open. They are nailed shut from the outside. He was very clever." A voice said from behind her. Sara turned to see the dead girl sitting up on her bed, the blood still dripping out of her wounds. He lifeless eyes seemed to look right through Sara. Sara screamed and rammed herself against the window. She would break the glass if she had to.

"You'll never make it. He planned this too well. The others that live here are loyal to him. They will help him to kill you. Just like they did for us." The dead girl said. Blood sprayed out of her mouth as she spoke but she didn't seem to notice. Sara tried not to look at her but felt a pulling sensation and her eyes were drawn back to the blood soaked girl on the bed. As soon as she made eye contact the lights went out again then flashed back on. The room was clean and the girl was gone. Then the door swung open. But the hall was empty. Sara poked her head out just enough to see her crew doing the same. They bolted towards the stairs only to see 24 bloody girls standing at the bottom staring up at them.

"He likes the chase. He likes the chase." They all chanted in a haunting harmony. Then they began climbing the stairs. They turned back to the hallway to see the man with the blade and the woman with the noose.

They moved towards them, slowly at first but then began to speed up, disappearing and reappearing closer and closer. Colin panicked and ran into the closest bedroom and slammed the door. Sara could him them trying to break the window. The woman with the noose smiled as she walked right through the door. There was a crashing sound then a thud. Then the door swung open slowly. Lila ran in to see if Colin had made it but as soon as she peered out the window she let out a horrible scream. She saw Colin swinging below from a noose. She turned back to look at her friends in horror but the door slammed shut once more and both phantoms were gone.

Seconds later there were terrible screams and then a gurgling sound. And once more the door swung open slowly. Lila was on the bed covered in her own blood with stab marks all over her body. Her eyes were looking up to the ceiling as if looking a God.

Sara almost ran into her but Matt grabbed her. He turned to look at the mob of dead sorority girls who stood staring with vacant expressions repeating, "He likes the chase."

"Help us!" He screamed. They ignored him. He grabbed Sara's arm and pulled her into the crowd.

"They aren't going to hurt us. They are his victims." He said and he and Sara ran down the stairs. Andrew couldn't move, he was frozen in fear. Andrew had never believed in the supernatural and couldn't process it. Matt and Sara ran to the front door and flung it open. Sara was about to yell for Andrew but at that very moment they saw a body drop from above the porch and swing in the same spot that Mary Lynch and Gary Lindale had hung themselves year before.

"Andrew!!!" Sara screamed. Matt dragged her to the car and fumbled with the keys. Finally he opened the doors and they both got inside and locked the doors. Sara looked at the house, now able to see it clearly in the moonlight. She saw Andrew's and Colin's bodies hanging from their nooses and looked up to the bedroom where Lila had been murdered. In the window stood the man with the knife. Next to him, stood a lifeless Lila. In all of the other windows, the Sorority sisters stood looking out into the night with their dead stares. Matt revved the engine and turned the van sharply to get back on the dirt road. That's when they saw the man with the truck. He stared at them. His gaze was unwavering. After a few moments he got in his truck and turned on his bright lights. Then he revved his engine and slammed on the accelerator. He was driving right at them.

"What the F*** is he doing?" Matt asked in shock. He didn't have time or room to get out of the way and Sara braced herself for the impact. But as soon as the truck would have touched the front fender, it disappeared. Matt looked around and in the rear view mirror. There was no sign of it.

"Just go!" Sara yelled.

And they did. They drove to the police station and told them everything that had happened. The police refused to go to the house until the morning and Matt and Sara stayed in their cell the rest of the night.

In the morning they all went back. It was just as they had left it. The police did their reports and the coroner was called. When they had gotten all their equipment out, Sara asked if they could leave. One of the cops agreed to take them back to their hotel and they climbed in the back of a car. Sara let her look once more at the big house. She looked up at the room where Lila had died. There in the window was Lila looking back at her. She waved a sad goodbye and disappeared.

Sara was institutionalized a week later and this is the only story she will ever tell.

DEAD AGAIN

ROBERT GATTO

21

"Sir, I need to speak with you urgently."

Doctor Zachary Jones straightened up from his microscope, rubbing his eyes and the back of his neck. He'd been working for the past fourteen hours without a break, with only a steady supply of coffee to keep him going. He was torn between being irritated at the interruption and relieved at the excuse to stop for a moment. His lab was silent, only the occasional distant scream could be heard echoing through the facility.

"What's up Mike?"

"The coroner from Zone 3 just couriered over a toxicology report from a recent murder victim, I think you should take a look at it."

Zach looked surprised at the statement. "He couldn't use email?"

Mike shook his head. "Signal's down again and the power's unstable. You're running on the backup generators but the rest of us are struggling with an intermittent supply again. God knows what the status is over in Zone 3. They're probably out altogether."

"I don't know if God has much to do with it anymore," Zach replied wryly. "I think we're on our own now."

Mike shrugged. "We're doing our best to rebuild things, but there just isn't enough people left to maintain everything, and not enough experts left for troubleshooting. We're still broadcasting the announcements over the air waves asking people to come, telling them we're offering employment, food and a place to stay, but nobody new has shown up for months. Contact with the scouting parties is obviously sketchy at best, but last we heard, they'd covered another seven states and hadn't found another living soul. It's looking like we gathered everyone up first time around."

"Dammit, we can't be the only people left in the whole of the United States! There's barely a thousand of us in each zone, that's less than six thousand people. With my contact with other bunkers before we lost them, I would estimate that the survivors at the time were in the region of thirty thousand at most. Last year, the population was three hundred and twenty *million*, and that was the ones that were registered and accounted for."

Mike sat down. "I know, it's crazy, the whole thing was a total shit storm, but right now, I need you look at this report."

"What's so special that a coroner can't handle his own murder case," Zach muttered, holding his hand out for the document. "It's not as if there's a lot of suspects left to choose from."

"I'd go straight to the toxicology report and look at the blood analysis if I were you," Mike advised.

Zach flipped the pages and finding the appropriate section, settled down to read. Ten minutes of silence ensued before Zach looked up with a panicked expression on his face.

"It can't be," he said helplessly.

"I was hoping I was wrong,"

It was the only answer Mike could give under the circumstances.

"Believe me, I'd have been happier to be interrupted for nothing, I can't believe this. I thought we'd wiped them out, apart from the ones we've got under lock and key."

To emphasize his point, another inhuman scream echoed through the underground facility where the public health department headquarters was now situated.

"You're absolutely certain that this is the same strain?"

"No doubt, but just in case we're acting like a couple of hysterical teenage girls, let's compare the print outs and double check."

After five minutes of silence while the two compared the reports, Zach stood. "We have to admit it, he was bitten or scratched by a zombie, he's infected with exactly the same strain of the virus that caused the first outbreak."

"That means there's still one out there, and we've led everyone to believe the streets are safe now."

"Not necessarily," Zach replied. "Is there any chance he's connected with research, that he would have been handling one of the captives for some reason? Maybe he just got careless."

"Afraid not, he was scanned completely clean before being dispatched to Zone 3, he's been working at the power plant ever since, trying to keep the grid up and running. That's where he was last seen."

"I hope everyone who handled the body stuck to procedure, else we've got another outbreak on our hands. Do you know if it's been incinerated yet?"

"The report doesn't say."

"Well for God's sake, find out, and make sure everyone who came into contact with this guy is thoroughly scanned. It's bad enough that there's still at least one running about out there, the last thing we need is the virus to be already on the inside."

"What are you going to do Zach?"

Zach sighed deeply. "First, I'm going to read this full report so I'm up on all the facts, after that, I've no idea."

Chapter Two

Zach maneuvered the motorbike through the city streets, carefully navigating what would have been a normal and noisy traffic jam but was now eerily silent and still. He'd decided that if he wanted a job done properly, he might as well do it himself. He was heading for Zone 3, but progress was slow. The cleanup operation that had been in place for months now were doing a good job of returning the city to a habitable state, but after the last of the zombies had been hunted down, all the remaining people found and scanned for the virus, they had been concentrating on removing bodies and incinerating them. Once that gruesome task was over, they'd begun on rubbish and rotting food, a huge problem since everyone's lives had been so suddenly and dramatically interrupted by the apocalypse that had hit them.

Half-eaten meals were left on tables, crawling with maggots and flies, fridges and freezers with no power were now filled with oozing mush which bore no resemblance to the groceries they'd once been, garbage cans and dumpsters crawled with rats and other vermin, omitting toxic stenches that polluted the very air around them. Zach shuddered to think of the stores and hypermarkets that had been filled with fresh produce. Yep, the cleanup crews had their work cut out for them, and they were making some pretty impressive headway, but they had more immediate worries than the graveyard of abandoned cars, trucks, vans and other vehicles that littered the roads, the result of the panic which had caused everyone to try and flee the city, hoping the virus was contained to one area and they could escape their fate.

Zach had initially hoped the same thing, but as a member of a government funded research team, he had been one of the first to hear that it was happening in every state countrywide, and spreading at a rate that no amount of forces could contain. The resulting loss of human life had been a greater tragedy than he could ever hope to express with mere words. He had gathered as much Intel as he could before lines of communication went down and it was every man for himself, isolated in their own small area. He and his team were aware of something most Americans were not, that every major city held at least one secure underground facility designed to protect the President in the event of terrorist attacks or natural disasters, wherever he may be at the time of their occurrence. Zach and his team had made their way there, with as much equipment as they could safely carry, moving rapidly under the cover of darkness and gathering up as many survivors as they could along the way. They sent out daily hunting parties, both to kill the zombies and to rescue as many of the human race as they could find uninfected. The bunker was designed to withstand anything anyone could possible imagine, and was stocked for the survival of hundreds for many years. Zach had immediately set up a broadcast over the airwaves giving detailed directions to safety. He also had the hunting parties place signs all over the city, begging people to come.

At first, people had arrived steadily. The bunker was spacious and equipped to outlast even nuclear radiation, but it had never been designed for so many. They had food and water, a state of the art medical facility and research lab, an extensive library, but what they lacked most severely was space. Living conditions became cramped and uncomfortable, so they had made plans to wipe out the threat and reclaim their society. They'd been through hardship and trauma, but through it, they had grown stronger. Some were already natural warriors, eager to unite and fight a common enemy, while others had to learn to ignore the horror and devastation they faced, overcoming their fears for the survival of the race. Zach was proud of each and every one. Slowly but surely, they had wiped out the zombies, taken the lives of those infected but not yet turned, and taken control of the city, gradually trying to return it to its former glory and reinstate all the systems that had been in place before the collapse of everything. Before communications went down, Zach had made contact with nine other bunkers across the country. They were occupied mostly by high level military personnel who had access codes, as many of their own teams that had survived, and rag tag bunches of survivors, just like Zach's own bunker. They had between them, coordinated a sweep of the USA with military precision, and had been in the midst of it when they lost contact. Only when Zach had completed his own instructions had he felt it safe for the people to return to life above ground, splitting the city into six manageable zones and allowing the people to choose their employment and place of residence.

Zach had worked tirelessly ever since, studying the virus, even requesting live samples of the creatures which were held in secure cages in the underground facility, in order to study them and to draw samples of blood and tissue to work with. He still had no idea where the virus had originated from, but his main purpose was to try and find a cure. Watching a loved one scream and beg for his life after being scanned positive for the virus, and having to ignore their pleas and end it for them before they could turn and infect others, was possibly the hardest thing to deal with throughout this horror. He was determined to put a stop to that, to find a cure that could halt the virus in its tracks and preserve the precious lives of the remaining few. His ultimate goal was one that could reverse it even after the infected had completely turned, but he'd settle for the first for now. Suddenly, he came across the sign that announced he was about to enter Zone 3, and he was surprised to find that he'd been lost in thought the whole journey. Concentrating now on the road, he headed for the crematorium which had been commandeered by the coroner to act as his new morgue, allowing for easy disposal of infected bodies. Nothing could be allowed to hang about for long these days.

Two guards stopped him at the door and he was required to remove his helmet and present some identification, only then was he allowed to pass. The coroner and the newly appointed chief of police were deep in conversation when he entered the room. Neither of them seemed surprised to see him. Zach didn't bother wasting time with pleasantries.

"Has the body been disposed of?"

"Of course," the coroner replied, shocked that he would be considered so incompetent as to not follow basic protocol.

"Good. Now gather up everyone, and I mean absolutely everyone, who had any contact with it at all, however minor."

"They've all been tested Zach," Pete, the chief of police told him gently.

"Yeah well, the virus can take a while to incubate and show itself. I'm testing them again."

"As you wish," Pete sighed, leaving to give the order.

"Might as well start with you Jimmy," Zach said, as he removed a pack of needles and a bulky handheld machine from his inside pocket. Reaching into the other side of his leather biker jacket, he removed a pack of gloves, a mask, a pair of goggles, and a batch of medical slides. He laid his equipment out on the desk and advanced on the coroner. Jimmy looked fearful as he rolled up his sleeve and presented his arm as Zach donned the safety equipment. He'd seen the gun strapped to Zach's hip as he'd pulled his jacket open, and he knew Zach wouldn't hesitate.

"I followed all the procedures," he whined as Zach drew a small amount of blood from his vein.

"Then you'll have nothing to worry about, will you?"

Zach proceeded to place a small drop of the blood on the slide, covered it with a sliver of membrane, and slid it into the machine. He pressed a few buttons then headed over to the bright yellow and black box marked for incineration and dropped the needle in. He returned and perched one hip on the edge of the desk, waiting for the machine to start throwing numbers at him. He had studied the virus extensively, he knew exactly the elevations and drops to look for to indicate that it was beginning to take hold, to slowly incubate, hiding in plain sight within its victim.

Jimmy was visibly sweating by the time Zach turned to him. "You're clean."

Jimmy sighed deeply with relief and swiped at his brow. "I'm the one who had most contact, I think testing the others is a waste of time and resources."

"Yeah, but the others might not have followed protocol as strictly as you. Look, Jim, we've got the same situation as we always had, people now concentrated again in the cities. You know how fast this happens, one infected person could wipe out all of Zone 3 in a matter of days or even hours, and you can bet your ass they'd move across the city searching for more food. The last thing you need is someone on the inside turning."

"I know, I know, it's better to be safe than sorry. It's just that they're all good men, I know each of them personally and I guess ... well, surviving this has created a bond ..."

Zach's expression softened. "I understand, I feel the same way, but until I can find a cure ..."

He left the rest of the words unspoken as the others began to enter the room. All of them were visibly relieved as they all tested clear of the virus that turned good men into drooling, slavering, mindless creatures that hungered for human flesh. They shuffled out of the room, no exuberance in their reprieve, only a thankfulness that left them almost weak with gratitude. Only Pete and Jimmy remained with Zach.

"Okay, so now that's over with, let's review this. The report said that the actual cause of death was a gunshot wound?"

"Yes, not an immediate kill shot, but he would have bled out within minutes," Pete replied.

"And nobody's coming forward to admit to the shooting?"

"We've questioned everybody and nobody seems to have any knowledge of it, and I believe 'em. The vic, Tom Smith, was last seen leaving the power plant at the end of his shift with his payment in food as usual. Reports all say he was same as ever, no weird moods, no unusual plans. He was found next morning by the Area West cleanup crew, who reported immediately. Location was on his way home but there was no sign of his food bag."

"So what's your theory?"

"Guess we got ourselves a lone drifter, who probably shot him for the food. We've been hunting but haven't managed to find him so he's probably moved on. I'm sending out an alert this morning to all areas to be on their guard and advise people not to carry food in plain sight."

"What about the bites?"

"There were only two, which is unusual, so my guess is that the creature was right there, getting in quick before Tom actually died. We know they don't eat dead flesh so I reckon it got the two bites in before he passed, then left him alone after that. I was hoping you could tell us why he didn't turn."

"Probably because he was so close to death and bleeding out," Zach shrugged. "The virus didn't have time to take hold and there wasn't enough blood still moving through the system to carry it."

"That makes sense," Jimmy interjected. "I had the same thoughts myself. I'm sorry he's dead but I'm glad he didn't turn into one of them."

"And you've found no sign of the creature either?"

"Nope, not a trace," Pete confirmed.

"Do you think it's possible the drifter and the zombie are one in the same? That maybe he was carrying the virus and turned just after the shooting?" Jimmy asked.

Zach considered the possibility. "It'd be one heck of a coincidence, but we know the virus takes about 48 hours to incubate fully and change the entire body, but when it does, it's almost instant. I guess it might be possible, he'd have been feeling pretty sick by then, maybe making him desperate enough to kill for food, putting his illness down to malnutrition or even starvation. But I'm not the only research facility with live samples, any reports of anybody losing one?"

"I sent people out to ask the very same question," Pete said. "So far, the ones that have come back have given a negative."

The three men digested the information in silence before Jimmy summed it up. "So either we've got a newly turned creature, or we've got one hell of a smart-assed zombie who's hiding out until opportunities arise."

"Either way, it's gotta be stopped or we'll have a second outbreak on our hands, and if it's one of our own guys, it'll retain some base memories of which areas of the city are active, and maybe even where the underground shelter is."

"Dear God, what are you gonna do, Zach."

"I'm gonna do what has to be done. Go out there and hunt the bastard down."

Chapter Three

Dressed as he was in head to toe black, biker leathers, from his heavy, buckled boots to his tight gloves, Zach looked more like a character from an action movie than the research scientist he was. The image was helped along with two guns at his side, held there by the holsters crossed over low on his hips. Another was concealed beneath his biker jacket in a shoulder holster and a long-range rifle was slung over his shoulder. In addition, his pockets bulged with ammo, and several knives were secured about his person.

"Are you still sure you want to do this alone? It wouldn't take more than a few hours to gather up and kit out a hunting party from all Zones. The military boys would handle this much better."

"We might not have hours, it's knocking off time soon and people are going to be on the streets heading home. This needs to be done now."

"At least let me come with you, it should be my job."

"Listen Pete, I know you mean well and I know you think you're better equipped for the job, and you're probably right, but if we're right in thinking this thing is deliberately hiding out and waiting for opportunities, then it's showing more intelligence than any of the others. Being alone might just offer it the opportunity it needs."

"So you're setting yourself up as bait?"

"If it comes to that, then yes, but hopefully I'll be bait that bites back."

"Just make sure you bite first."

Zach looked at Pete with a serious expression. "If I fail, I can rely on you to do the right thing?"

Pete returned his steady gaze. "I'd advise you keep the helmet on at all times, but if you get bitten or scratched, just make sure you take it off before you turn so we have a clear and clean head shot."

"Understood."

The men shook as they parted, each wondering if they would ever see the other again. Once out on the street, Zach checked his watch. The power plant was the largest place of employment in Zone 3 and there would be a shift change soon, he intended to be there, watching and following people home. They'd all been advised to travel in groups and carry weapons at all times, but there were always some that wouldn't heed the advice. If the thing was going to show itself, he wanted to be there to meet it.

He slid his leg over the bike, negotiating the panniers that had been added. One was filled with extra ammo for all his weapons, the other contained fresh water, a few energy bars and a walkie talkie in case he needed assistance out on the road. He could have done without the food, he could survive longer without it than the zombie would take to find another victim. If he began to starve before he had killed it, it would be all over for them anyway. The bike gave a powerful roar as he shot off into the growing dusk to head to the power plant.

Zach sat and watched from the shadows as people began to spill from the plant, talking and joshing each other as people who closely work together every day tend to do. It gave Zach a pang of sadness, it felt like a distant memory from a past life, something safe, something normal. At first, the people stuck to various groups as instructed, not quite as alert to their surroundings as Zach would have hoped, but at least heeding some of the warning. Zach followed on foot, and as the groups split to head in different directions, he tried to decide which one to stick with. He assessed them quickly. One group contained a guy that was on the outskirts, hanging back and not joining in the general conversation. Making his decision, Zach jogged back for the bike.

He'd quickly made it back and sure enough, the guy had split, walking off on his own down another street. Zach had figured him for a loner and as such, he'd probably picked a building to live in that didn't have any other occupants. He couldn't blame the guy, they'd all thought they were safe. Zach parked up the bike again and followed on foot, keeping to the shadows. He was relieved and disappointed when the guy made it safely to a large apartment building with no incident. The outer door was locked, and Zach caught a glimpse of the heavy steel reinforcement on the inside as the man unlocked it then swung it open and darted inside. He heard several locks and deadbolts click into place behind the man.

The loner was home safe, but Zach couldn't give up on the nagging feeling that he wouldn't be the only one to think he was the best chance for a zombie dinner. He decided to take a wander around the neighbourhood and see what he could throw up. With no real clue as to where to start, it seemed as good as any other. With the streets completely devoid of human life, Zach found himself with nothing to do but think as he walked and watched.

He had figured out a lot about the virus, but still didn't really understand it. The body seemed to be dead, the heart no longer beat, the organs didn't function, the flesh itself was dead, feeling no hot or cold, no pain, no injury too great to ignore completely. Yet they weren't dead in the sense we normally understood. To create that desire, that need for flesh, that never ending, driving hunger, synapses in the brain had to be firing. It was this that brought around the rudimentary intelligence, the memory patterns and the social interaction. He had watched them closely in captivity. They recognized their own new, strange species, accepted one another and even formed close bonds with some around them. They were protective of each other, and when given food, it might look like a horrendous, violent frenzy but if you looked closer, there was order to it and it was ensured that everyone got a partial share of what was available. As he'd watched, Zach had determined that more and more of the brain had seemed to fire up again over time, the sparks of certain areas kick starting others. Their intelligence increased the longer they survived. His main question now was whether the body would rot and fail before they regained full intelligence. If it didn't, even the ones in captivity posed a serious risk and would have to be destroyed, cutting Zach off from his research material.

He wasn't sure what he was dealing with here, but it seemed unlikely to be an older zombie, it had attacked the dying man too quickly. That seemed to imply one fairly recently formed, which meant to go undetected as it had, it had retained much more of the thinking process. Zach was pulled from his inner musings by a rustling noise from behind a set of dumpsters up ahead. He walked forward with more caution. If it was from inside, it was most likely rats. The vermin had survived and thrived on the rot and decay left behind by the people ripped from their daily lives. As he approached, he determined that the noise was coming from behind the bins, not inside.

He pulled one of the guns from the holster, releasing the safety and chambering a bullet, readying the gun to fire. He crept forward as quietly as he could in his heavy boots and flipped his visor down, protecting his eyes from possible infected blood spray or grasping, gouging fingers. He ducked down as he reached the bins, using them as cover as he slid along the front and round the side. He paused there, steadying his breathing and preparing himself for what he might find. With one final exhale, he turned the corner, gun raised, finger poised on the trigger.

A stray dog looked up at him and snarled, head low, a deep, menacing growl forming in its throat. It advanced one step, protecting whatever disgusting meal it had found. Zach almost laughed with relief but didn't want to be forced to shoot the dog if he caused it to attack. Other than the vermin and bugs that bred at rapid rates, animals were a scarce commodity in this new world. One day, this half-starved mutt might once again be someone's companion, their comfort in a lonely existence. He stepped away, allowing the animal to grab its prize and scarper.

He had surmised from his research and information that the virus didn't seem to effect any other species of life, although test subjects had been hard to come by. There were no reports or any zombie animals among the cities and those few he had captured to inject directly with infected blood had shown no ill effects and after a few months of observation, he had been able to release them with no concerns about the safety of the survivors. Similar reports from more rural areas with a wider range of species had confirmed their suspicions that it was only humans that turned. However, animals did seem to suffice as a meal for the zombies when they couldn't get to human flesh, but Zach had yet to fully understand their need to eat, since it didn't seem to sustain them in any way. It was just another piece of the puzzle, and hopefully, he would stay alive to solve it. His relieved reaction to the first tense moment had reminded him just how ill-equipped he was for his current task, his only advantage his basic understanding of the creatures he had been studying.

Chapter Four

Throughout the night, Zach searched, covering what he could working in an ever increasing circle out from the power plant, still certain that the concentration of people and the constant presence of human flesh was what had drawn the creature into Zone 3. He used the bike to cruise the streets, then would return to likely looking buildings to hunt through them. Despite his importance as a research scientist, he had not excluded himself from the original hunting parties so was not without some acquired skills, but every time he entered a building, he felt like a young boy poking a hornet's nest, aware of the danger he was stirring up but too intent on his purpose to stop.

As dawn rose, the only thing of interest he'd found was a recent camp, the empty food tins scattered around letting him know it belonged to a human, possibly the drifter that had shot Tom Smith. That was one for the police chief, he would report it later, if and when more pressing matters were resolved. Feeling the need to relieve himself after his long night, he headed to one of the many abandoned service stations. He wasn't sure which buildings had a water supply in Zone 3, so best to use a public urinal rather than a bathroom in a private residence and be unable to flush, the city had enough problems.

He entered cautiously, stepping over the fallen shelves and scattered goods that remained, mostly motor oils and cleaning products for cars that no longer ran or couldn't be negotiated through the blocked up streets and highways even if they did have some fuel left in the tank. Shattered glass and spilled produce littered the floor, evidence of the panicked raids that had taken place in the early days, and he crunched his way across them, aware he was making too much noise but unable to find a clear path to the back where the restroom was located. He stopped halfway, pausing to see if his presence had attracted any attention. Silence.

He moved on and pushed open the restroom door. It groaned on hinges stiff from lack of use and Zach entered. The small corridor was pitch black as the door swung closed behind him and he scrambled for his flashlight, sighing in relief as the beam showed the corridor still empty. Locating the door to the men's room, he was more prepared, removing one of his guns and readying it. With both hands occupied, he pushed the door open with his shoulder, almost expecting a screaming, snarling face to appear the moment it opened. He had created the image so clearly in his mind he was almost surprised when nothing happened. The room itself had high windows which provided natural light from the rising sun so he clicked off his flashlight and tucked it safely back into his pocket. One by one, he checked the stalls, not wishing to be taken by surprise while he was otherwise occupied. The room was clear.

Zach was relieved to step back outside, buildings held no sense of safety or security any more. Instead, they provided too many places to hide, too many dark, shadowy areas where danger could lurk undetected or where you could end up cornered and trapped, the safe haven becoming a tomb. He gave an involuntary shiver, recalling the early days when screams of rage and terror, both human and inhuman, were all that could be heard from wherever you tried to hide. He was still incredulous that he and most of his team, all scientists focused on their research, distracted and not even equipped to live in the real world, had made it through this. He removed his helmet and retrieved a bottle of water from the pannier, leaning against the bike as he took a big swig, still contemplating his own dumb luck. He couldn't help but wonder if the survivors, himself included, had got too cocky, too confident of their success. Suddenly, from the corner of his eye, he thought he spotted movement.

Zach turned quickly and saw the figure of a male in the distance. The man too had stopped in his tracks on spotting Zach and for a second, they stared at one another. The figure was large, almost six foot tall, broad at the shoulders and from what Zach could make out, was dressed in army fatigues. As it didn't scream and make its way towards him, Zach figured it was somebody from the Zone out on a routine patrol, but the way he was staring made Zach nervous. He raised his hand in a wave of greeting and his movement broke the spell between them. Zach's water bottle fell from his hand as the man turned to run, and gave away the uneven, clumsy, loping gait of a zombie.

Zach immediately gave chase, cursing himself for having the rifle jammed along the side of the bike, unready to fire, and for all the guns having their safeties on. He had taken too many precautions and now they slowed him down as he fumbled with one of the hand guns as he ran. The creature had disappeared around a corner, and as Zach skidded round the same one, he came to a halt. The street was empty. He examined the buildings on either side, all apartment blocks by the looks of it. It could be inside waiting in any one. Zach took several steps down the street, careful to stick to the middle of the road. Up ahead, he could see a dead end, explaining why the road was devoid of abandoned vehicles, only a few parked cars sat at the side of the road in allocated parking bays. It had to have ducked inside a building on this street, the wall at the end was too high and smooth to scale. He gave himself time to wonder at the intelligence of that move. Perhaps he was mistaken? Maybe this was just a man surviving out here on his own. An injury could have caused the awkward gait and Zach hadn't really been close enough to tell one way or another.

"Hello," he called out. "Is anyone there? I'm not looking to hurt anyone, I'm hunting a creature, not a person."

Other than his voice echoing, there was no reply. It occurred to Zach that this person might be the drifter who'd shot and killed Tom Smith. If that was the case, Zach was a sitting duck out here. He didn't carry food, but his weapons and bike would certainly be worth killing for. He moved closer in towards the parked cars, hoping they would give some cover if anyone opened fire on him. He continued to move down the street, slowly, turning every few steps to ensure he kept an eye on every approach, glancing up at windows as he did so. He slowed as he came upon a car with the sidewalk side doors and trunk partially open.

He tried to peer into the car as he approached but his vision was obstructed by the sun glinting off the windshield. He reached the hood, sliding his way along the side of the car, both hands gripping the handle of the gun. He could see now that the front was empty and the back seats appeared that way too. Didn't mean to say someone wasn't hiding on the floor in the back. He move further forward, allowing himself a better view. The car was empty. He took a deep breath and steeled himself to check the trunk. Once again, an image filled his mind, a man hiding there, on his back, gun at the ready, Zach's face blown to smithereens by repeated shots the minute he stepped round and raised the trunk. He pushed it away and moved fast, intending to fire the first shot. His plan might have worked, but he was left staring at the bullet hole through the bottom of the empty trunk, the sound of his shot ringing in his ears, blocking out the sound of the door to his right opening. The next thing he knew, something slammed into him, sending him flying into the middle of the road where he stumbled and fell.

Chapter Five

Face down on the ground, Zach heard the inhuman, guttural scream and he scrambled to turn around to face his assailant. His leathers had saved him from any injury during the fall, but he'd lost his grip on the gun, which had skittered across the road out of his reach. He didn't have time to retrieve another as the creature was almost upon him. As Zach stared at the hollow, almost skeletal face, the dripping, slavering jaws and the tattered army clothing, he was left in no doubt what he was facing this time. He felt frozen, like a rabbit in headlights as it lumbered towards him, favoring its left leg.

Breaking his fear-induced paralysis, Zach bent both knees and waited, using every inch of his inner resolve not to attempt to get to his feet in the few nanoseconds he had before it reached him. Poised, he waited. As the creature reached and bent forward with its anxious maw, Zach kicked as hard as he could, landing his heavy boots dead center on the monster's chest, sending it staggering backwards, flailing its arms to keep its balance. Zach got up and advanced, the zombie meeting his attack head on, showing an inordinate amount of strength as they grappled, Zach attempting to bring the creature to its knees. The creature attempted to get at his face, the only exposed part of his body, his leathers protecting him from the long, ugly scratching talons and the snapping jaw as they fought and punched.

Finally, Zach managed to take advantage of the weaker leg, another hefty kick to the knee dropping the half man, half animal. Zach quickly applied the handcuffs provided to him by Pete before he set out, intending to retrieve them after the deed was done. The creature knelt there, head down, arms behind its back, silent, as if it already knew what fate awaited it. Zach stood in front of it as he removed the second handgun from his hip holster. The metallic snaps and clicks of him preparing the gun to fire echoed back from the empty buildings around them. He raised his arm, carefully aiming the gun at the bent head in front of him, taking his time in hopes of a quick, clean kill.

"Don't."

Zach stared, hardly able to believe what he thought he had just heard, his expression almost comically incredulous. "What? Did you just ... *say* something?"

"Please ... don't ...shoot."

The voice was hoarse and cracked, like an old man left abandoned in a neglectful nursing home that'd had no occasion to use it for many years, the words uncertain, hesitant. This was impossible! The basic level of brain activity that remained after the virus had wreaked its havoc was not enough for speech. He had seen some of the older ones communicate only with uncoordinated touches and basic grunts, and he'd had no reason to believe it would ever advance beyond this. Scientific curiosity overcame him, and he studied the creature more closely. Judging by the clothes and the state of the body, it wasn't old, had only turned a month or two ago at most, there was no way it should have regained this level of intelligence so fast. Despite feeling ridiculous, he spoke in return.

"Why shouldn't I?"

The creature raised its head and Zach gasped. Yes, the hollow face and dripping jaws screamed monster, but the eyes! They weren't the usual empty, staring voids of nothingness he'd come to expect. They were dark brown, and in them, he could read emotions, anger, sorrow, despair, he saw them all flicker within. Slowly, the gun began to drop.

"Help me," it pleaded, the words barely formed around the swollen, blackish tongue.

"What are you?" Zach asked, more to himself than anyone else, not really expecting an answer.

"Infected."

Zach put his gun away and knelt down on the ground beside the creature. It shrank away.

"Too close, can't stop."

Zach backed up a little. "Are you telling me that you don't want to hurt me but you can't help yourself? That the urge is to strong."

The creature nodded and turned it's large, dark eyes upon him, pleading and longing at the same time.

"Do you remember how you were infected?"

"Remember ... everything."

Dear God! Zach struggled to get his head around the possibility, how it would feel to remember everything about you that was human and right, yet be trapped inside a body that craved to rip and tear at human flesh, the urges too great to ignore. This man was in a special kind of hell and part of Zach told him to put the thing out of its misery, but the scientist in him couldn't listen. This was something different. For some reason, the virus hadn't eradicated the man inside, and he needed to know why.

"Listen to me, I can try to help you, but you need to help me. I need to take you back to my lab. I need to study you, your brain, your blood, your tissue. I'm trying to find a cure, will you come back with me?"

"Bite."

"Yeah, okay, I get it. You'll bite me at any opportunity. Guess the bike's out of the question then."

Zach looked around, wondering what to do. He wished he'd decided to carry the walkie talkie with him and not leave it with the bike, but he hadn't really anticipated a use for it other than if he needed to report in for a team to come and kill him before he turned. There was no one in sight that could help, and even if there were, he would be reluctant to enlist their services. They would want to kill this thing in front of him straight away, seeing only one of the abominations that had almost wiped out civilization, not understanding the importance it might have. His team were the only ones who could be trusted. Zach had no choice but to get back to the bike and retrieve the walkie talkie. He turned to the kneeling zombie.

"Wait here, I'll be back in a sec."

With no reason to believe the creature would obey, Zach sprinted back to where he had left the bike. He grabbed the radio and turned it on, calling back to Zone 3 base and putting in a request for them to get Mike to contact him on a certain frequency. He left the radio on, its volume turned to high, and slipped it inside his top pocket. Spotting his motorcycle helmet sitting on the seat where he had left it, he snatched it up before racing back to the spot he had left the zombie. To his great relief, it was still there, kneeling in the middle of the road. Zach rushed up behind it, slamming the full-faced helmet on over its head and buckling it tightly under the chin. It didn't even try to fight and seemed to gladly accept Zach's help to get to its feet. With its mouth covered and hands still cuffed behind its back, Zach began the long walk back to Zone 1, hoping the call from Mike would come soon. Just because the creature was docile right now didn't mean it would remain that way. Perhaps the human side was in charge right now, and that could shift at any moment. As unprecedented as this way, there was no way to tell. He'd already had a taste of how strong it was, if it chose to fight, he'd given it a weapon and protection by putting the helmet on.

They'd been walking for about thirty minutes when the radio sparked to life inside his pocket. He paused, letting go of the hold he had on the cuff chain to answer it.

"Mike, I'm at the crossroads of," Zach glanced around, looking for street signs. "Jefferson Avenue and Lincoln Drive. Can you plot a route to get a car through to pick me up? I've got a live one I need to bring in."

"Sure," the voice crackled on the other end. "I'll get the army boys out to you."

"No, no army, not this time. You know they hate me keeping the things alive. Any resistance and they'll shoot to kill, and I really need this one."

"Fine, but it might take me a while to get to you. I don't know the roads like those boys."

"That's okay, we'll head along Jefferson and keep moving west, just find us as soon as possible."

"Will do. Be careful."

Zach tucked the radio away and carried on walking. An hour later, he'd never been more relieved to hear the sound of an engine in his life.

Chapter Six

The journey passed without incident, except for Mike's pure disbelief at what Zach had found. Unwilling to make the back seat passenger act like a performing monkey, he'd refrained from conversing with it just to prove himself right for Mike's benefit. He would see soon enough. As they pulled up as close to the entrance of the underground facility as they could, Zach wondered if he should have blindfolded the creature as an extra precaution, just in case it should escape. Figuring he was too late, the two men went ahead with the transfer.

Suddenly, the thing decided it'd had enough and both were thankful for not only the motorcycle helmet they'd left in place, but also the army personal who heard the guttural screams from below and came running to assist. It took four of them and the scientists to get the enraged zombie into a cell and sedated.

"This one should be eradicated immediately, it's too strong," the one in charge declared, glowering at Zach.

"It's caged now, its fine. Thanks for your help, we can take it from here."

With one last uncertain look, the military personnel left the two men alone with the zombie. Zach had taken the precaution of placing it alone, unsure of how the others would react to it. He was afraid they would recognize it as different from them and attack it.

"There's no way that thing spoke to you, you must have been hallucinating. Lack of sleep, dehydration..."

"I know what it looks like, Mike, but how do you think I managed to get it restrained and the helmet on if it didn't let me? You've seen how strong he is."

"Oh, so it's a he now? Zach, you're losing the plot."

"Just please trust me and help me out here. The army personnel are already making noises about not keeping him, that he's too strong to be safe. If they get any inkling as to how intelligent it is, I won't be able to reason with them. Stay with him, and when he comes round, tell him to keep it hidden except from you and me, okay?"

"Sure, I'll sit and chat with the flesh eating zombie, no problem."

Mike was disgruntled and still disbelieving, but Zach knew he'd come around once he saw what he'd seen, and he knew he'd do as he'd been asked. Secure in the knowledge that his new acquisition was safe for the moment, he headed into his lab with the blood he had drawn from him once the sedation had taken effect. Putting a drop on a slide, he inserted into the same type of machine he's used and left behind at Zone 3 the day before. He waited impatiently for the results to collate, then watched in amazement as for the first time the machine let him down. The read out on the display screen was going haywire, unable to settle on any figures, the numbers changing every few seconds until they became such a blur, Zach could no longer read them.

"Must be faulty," he muttered, whishing he hadn't left the other one behind.

He placed another drop of blood on a fresh slide and slid it under his microscope. Focusing the delicate piece of equipment, he couldn't quite believe what he was seeing. On the slide, a war was raging. Healthy, human cells were under attack from ones already affected by the virus, but just as fast, the normal cells were fighting back, almost eradicating the virus completely before being overcome once again. The man's entire bloodstream must be a mass of constantly changing and adapting cells.

"No wonder the machine went nuts!" Zach murmured, his thoughts already racing as to how to identify what this man's blood contained that allowed it to fight the infection. If he could pinpoint it and enhance it, he was not only well on the way to finding a cure, but he could also create a vaccine for immunity against the virus. As long as he had a supply of this man's blood long enough to figure it all out, he could ensure the survival of the human race and prevent this ever happening again.

Jubilant, he dashed from the lab, hardly able to contain himself, desperate to share the news with Mike and get him working on it with him straight away. He didn't pause when he heard the half-human scream echoing in the corridors, he was used to that. When the following rally of gunshots rang out in response, Zach stopped in his tracks. Mike came down the corridor with an apologetic look on his face, a deep scratch down his left cheek.

"I'm sorry," Mike said. "I'm so sorry. He spoke to me Zach, he actually spoke! Intelligent conversation. My God! I couldn't believe it. I let my guard down, Zach, I got too close. I've let you down."

An armed army officer stepped round the corner, his weapon aimed at Mike. He spoke into a radio clipped to his shirt. "Subject one neutralized, subject two in my sights."

Zach dropped to his knees and sobbed.

END

OUR DEAD BODIES

by Jerry Wright

The ax felt heavier in his hand than it did when he chopped wood every autumn for the winter. He knew the weight was emotional and not physical but there was still something contradictory about the ease with which it arced over his shoulder and closed the distance to the teenager's head. She didn't have a great deal of hair left, and he wondered briefly if that had anything to do with how effortlessly it seemed to cleave her skull. She crumpled to the ground in front of him. The ax didn't travel with her but her body simply slid off in a sadly anticlimactic way. He had to sidestep because his grip had loosened and the ace head swung down and toward him.

She was dead and—

Could he call her that? If the unnaturalists were right, she died weeks or even months ago. Hell, if the unnaturalists were right, the immediate guilt and self-loathing that washed over him was inappropriate and wasted emotion. He felt it, though.

She couldn't have been older than fifteen when she was... alive? He didn't quite buy the theory that the girl hadn't been alive before the ace fell. If not death, then what? Trauma, yes. Resurrection, maybe. Some kind of resurrection unlike everything promised. There was no glorious new body, no virgins, no cavorting with the gods. There was only an ace that cleaved too easily and belied the significance of the end.

He didn't know if she lived before the ace fell or if she was dead. In any case, that part of her life in which she was rational couldn't have lasted for more than fifteen years. Perhaps that part of her life ended months ago, perhaps as long as a year ago. Every part of her life was over now.

He leaned against the ace, resting the head on the ground. He wanted to wipe the blade on the grass but he couldn't come up with the energy, couldn't come up with any energy at all. She wasn't bleeding. That part of the whole mess was the most disturbing. . Somehow, the fact that blood didn't seep from her and pool around her made everything seem hopeless along with violent. It made the loathing seem contradictory as well but that didn't mitigate it at all. It seemed wrong, and he wished he could somehow make the death more visibly significant, less like killing a prop

A sudden rustling in the trees to the left of the campsite startled him and the ace instantly came back up as he whirled toward the noise. Two men stepped forward.

Men, alive in every sense.

They held shotguns, and when they saw him, the guns lowered. "You got her for us, then," one said amicably.

He let the ace return to the ground and sighed. "You were hunting her?"

"Yes," the man replied. He was short, ruddy faced, and wearing camouflage he'd probably bought from an army surplus store years before everything went to hell. The companion was thin and mousey. Images of the old cartoon with the big bulldog and the tiny terrier leaping around it in sycophantic bliss came to mind and he resisted the urge to make a comment. "Good thing you knew how to take care of business. I guess we drove her this direction." The man smiled and rolled his eyes. He shook his head and lifted his hands almost apologetically. "Her? Hell. It." He stepped forward slightly and said, "Green. Donovan Green." The man nodded to the other. "That's Sean Arcineaux."

"Hal North. Lot of them out here?" Hal was true. North was not.

"Not anymore. We patrol these parts for Spring Kettle. You from Spring Kettle?" Hal shook his head and Green continued. "Little town about eight miles down the road. About two-thousand survivors." *Survivors.* The world was mostly survivors, and towns like Spring Kettle probably only had a dozen or so to address in the first place. Hal nodded anyway and hoped he seemed impressed, raising an eyebrow slightly.

Green seemed happy. He seemed ecstatic. Hal wondered how many hours he'd prepared for the job with an energy drink in one hand and a video game console controller in the other. Green finally found his calling and Hal wondered if he were proud because it had only taken a tragedy of biblical proportions. He sighed again and nodded toward the girl's body but Green asked, "Where you from?"

"Dallas." He wasn't from Dallas. He knew, though, that Dallas had suffered more than any other city so that some neighborhoods lay in ruins. "Not sure where I'll go next."

"Spring's not a bad place."

"I'm going to head north. Got family in South Dakota." Another lie. He expounded on it. "No idea if they're still alive."

Green nodded. "Yeah. They ruined everything." It wasn't true. Humanity did. "You okay here? We only saw signs of this one but there could be more around."

"I'll be okay. My car has a full tank. I think I'll just pack up and head North."

"We'll burn the body. Otherwise it'll attract others."

Hal nodded. "I have some lighter fluid in the car."

"One day all of these fucking zombies will be dead," Green said.

Hal winced. He hated the word. Green's expression changed and Hal shook his head and said, "They destroyed everything. Hope that day comes soon."

Green nodded. "And life can go back to normal." Hal was pretty sure nothing on Earth would make Green unhappier. He didn't answer but went to the back of his car, opened the trunk, and pulled out the bottle of fluid. He saw his shogun in there and picked it up, too, pumping a round into the chamber. He paused and closed his trunk just as Green cried out, "Jesus! Look out! There are two in your car!"

Hal felt the familiar sickness crash over him as he brought the shotgun up and fired. Green's head exploded in red mist. Arcineaux screamed but Hal's second shot brought him down. Hal walked over to Green and looked down sadly on him. Most of his head was gone. This time, there was plenty of blood.

He stared at Green's body for a long time and wondered why he'd been more troubled after killing the teenager than now. He was still troubled but there was no guilt, no loathing. He turned around and opened the car door. "It's okay, Honey," he said. "You and Kaylee can come out now."

***

"We'll leave them," he said. "We just don't have time."

He waited as she nodded, an excruciatingly slow process now though the comprehension showed in her eyes immediately. He'd spent the first months fighting the urge to finish sentences or otherwise hurry the conversation along.

They weren't rotting. Not yet. Maybe they wouldn't. There were theories abounding about all of that. Of course, the unnaturalists wouldn't hear about it. To them, they would rot because they were dead and their bodies were unnatural. Others, those who held to the virus theory no matter how many times it was debunked, portrayed it all as mind over matter, as the minds convinced the bodies they were dead. Others, primarily those who debunked the virus theory, claimed it was a mutated version of leprosy, and the rotting occurred at an accelerated rate simply because of the inability to feel pain and thus address small wounds. Somehow, the bacteria caused encephalitis in some and not in others, so some became violent and some didn't.

Hal thought that last theory the most likely but it didn't account for the sudden outbreak in various geographical regions. The lack of pain was real, though. He'd seen Kaylee slice the palm of her hand on a jagged piece of metal, seen her keep playing with no indication she felt any pain at all. He'd scrubbed the wound and bound it and then taken a book on leprosy from the library, wistfully wishing the government, which undertook heroic efforts to keep certain institutions in place, would have done the same for libraries. Knowledge would certainly be lost in a generation unless the growing anarchy somehow slowed.

The books stressed something called visual surveillance of extremities, VSE, as a means to prevent rot. Evidently, the key to living with leprosy was scanning your fingers and toes constantly and by doing so catch any small cuts for treatment before they became infected. Of course, Kaylee and Lori couldn't do it themselves. That meant he had to constantly survey their extremities. It was habit now, Hal guessed, as they removed themselves from the car and helped him pack up the campsite.

They were still them.

He saw it less and less lately but they were there beneath whatever dullness the condition brought. They were there behind the strange, pinkish pupils that revealed their condition to Green and Arcineaux. They were there, and so far outside of their eyes their bodies still seemed like them. He knew they were there. Mannerisms remained that proved it, the way Lori inclined her head and sighed when Kaylee frustrated her even if the phrase "Young lady, don't make me ask again" had shortened to "Young lady, don't" in a long, low sentence that took three times as long as the original. Kaylee still climbed in his lap to say, "Please, Daddy!" even if the journey took her a minute or two and the words were barely recognizable.

The unnaturalists were winning.

They were winning and it was open season on the infected, which Hal guessed made a lot of sense to some. The violent infected behaved just like the movies, not moving like the creatures with that weird shuffle but still killing and some even eating their victims. The unnaturalists were winning but there was no distinguishing between the violent infected and those who weren't.

Hal took the bodies of the two men and placed them with the teenage girl. She'd been violent, beyond hope. At least, she'd been beyond help. He took their weapons along with their ammunition and put it all in the trunk, returning with the lighter fluid and dousing their bodies. Between the two of them, Kaylee and Lori had managed to pull the tent's spikes out of the ground. He sighed, squirted some lighter fluid on a twig, and lit it with his lighter. He dropped the makeshift match onto the bodies and, satisfied with the minor inferno that resulted, walked to help with the camp. He let them work on the tent and instead packed up the little stove and the mesh grill for the campfire. Those, too, he put in the trunk.

He considered letting them finish the tent. Even though she couldn't communicate it, he knew Lori felt bitterly disappointed when he had to help her with a simple task. He grew too worried about it, though, too concerned others would come for Green and Arcineaux. He walked to the tent and put his hand on Lori's arm. "Honey. Let me do the tent. Can you and Kaylee throw sticks and branches on the bodies?" Lori nodded, her pink pupils seemed to dilate for a moment, and then she turned and walked to Kaylee. She moved slowly, more slowly than she had before. Still, it wasn't at all like the lumbering monsters from the movies. He watched her for a moment.

She was still beautiful.

She was still beautiful and he hadn't touched her for six months.

He'd wanted to. Of course he'd wanted to. They'd been active, very active, prior to Hell descending to Earth or rising up on Earth or however the damned metaphor worked. They'd gone at it like rabbits for the first year of their marriage and still went at it for most of the pregnancy. Lori became aggressive only a few months after Kaylee was born, and they'd been rabbits again. Nine years they'd been rabbits. Now they didn't do a thing, and he didn't know if he was supposed to do something or if she would or if it hurt her or if she'd be hurt by it.

He was pretty sure she wanted it. Even with all the changes, he could sometimes catch a wistful expression on her face, the one that replaced the almost placid kind of blankness that seemed to characterize their outward emotions if not their inward. He wondered if he should just do it. They would have no trouble finding an abandoned hotel on the road and there ought to be one with adjoining rooms. He could get Kaylee occupied and just do it. She felt unattractive to him plenty of times before all this. Perhaps that was the issue. Perhaps she thought he didn't want her. He could sleep with her to reassure her.

Yeah. Of course that could all be rationalization.

When the car was packed, he used the rest of the lighter fluid to make sure the bodies and branches would keep burning. Despite all of the predictions, things weren't too hard to come by. There had been some hoarding in the beginning but when people realized not enough of society had been destroyed to upend everything, the hoarding slowed down. Production had slowed for everything, stopped for most things. Really, though, that only meant there weren't a lot of pre-packaged snack chips. Vegetables and meat were still plentiful, sold mostly from little stands rather than giant mega stores.

Why did he do that? Why did he do everything he could to pretend the end of the world hadn't come? Why did he do so much justification? *Sure, everything got blown the fuck back to the Old West but hey, all the movies acted like we'd be back in the Stone Age.* There wasn't a lot of comfort with it but it helped him keep up the hatred for the people who would kill Kaylee and Lori, the people who walked around like road warriors in a world that, if anything, had plenty of gas and water left.

"Medicine." It took Lori almost ten seconds to say the word, and though he understood what she wanted he waited until she was finished and then nodded. He wondered if it made a difference to her, him not jumping ahead but waiting. He opened the bag in the trunk and pulled out three pills for each of them. Rifampicin was a leprosy drug. He'd taken it from an abandoned pharmacy. They didn't have the other two drugs used to treat it but he knew they were all antibiotics. The other pills were just antibiotics. He had bottles full of different varieties that all ended with *cyllin*. If it all really did come down to bacteria, maybe it was helping.

Lori swallowed the pills and then made Kaylee swallow hers. Hal closed the trunk. "We should get on the road now, Honey," he said. She nodded and got Kaylee settled. It was inefficient. Hal could have strapped in her much faster but he believed Lori needed it. When she finished, Lori closed the car door and began her slow walk to the other side. "Would you like to ride up front? If we see a car, you'll have to pretend you're sleeping."

She smiled. At least, he thought she smiled. There definitely seemed to be at least a small upturn in the corners of her mouth. He intercepted her on the way to the door and pulled her to him, holding her tightly. He felt her arms tighten on him as well and had to fight back tears. He pulled back slightly and kissed her forehead. "I love you," he whispered.

He held her through the minute or so it took her to say that she loved him too.

***

The road was lonely. It felt strange to know they would likely drive for hours without seeing another car even though humanity hadn't become devastated into little pockets of survivors like all the films. People tended to stay close, though, tended to treat everywhere outside of their particular environment as wilderness. He glanced at the gas tank. They had a quarter tank, and the dashboard told him that was good for another hundred and seventeen miles. Gas wasn't much of a problem. There were still gas stations working in the larger cities and still pipelines and refineries keeping it going. Demand had dropped dramatically, though, and he filled his tank far more often from an abandoned vehicle than at a pump.

He glanced at Lori. She sat with her eyes closed and he wondered if she did that just to make sure her limited ability to react quickly wouldn't lead to their discovery. She rarely slept anymore, perhaps an hour or two per night. He looked at the rear view mirror. Kaylee's pink eyes stared forward. She noticed him looking and took an eternity to smile. He smiled back and scanned the horizon for a place to stop. Dusk, almost.

The mountains had already given way to a long stretch of plains, the kind of Southwest stretch that meant tiny towns that abruptly changed the speed limit from seventy-five miles per hour to thirty-five. Most of those towns were empty now, citizens more comfortable in heavier pockets of population, citizens more comfortable with authorities killing the infected so they didn't have to. As though the highway itself heard him, a sign came up, advertising Honey Blossom Rock as forty-two miles away. "Ready to stop for the night, Kaylee?" he asked.

It took a long time for her to get out a reply, and it took him a moment to realize she was asking him for ice cream when they got there. He hoped there was some left in one of the stores. He said, "We'll see," and then slowed because there was a semi-truck on the side of the road up ahead. It looked like it might be from the seventies and he thought that meant there was a chance for gas rather than diesel. He could take diesel, use it for lighting fires or something along those lines but it wouldn't fuel the car. He pulled beside it and Lori wasn't sleeping because her eyes opened when the car stopped. "I'm going to see if I can fill the tank," he said.

She managed to say, "Okay," and this time it was difficult to hide his impatience because in this new world—*Brave New World*, he thought bitterly—stopping in an unfamiliar place was dangerous. He held back, though, and remained in his seat until she finished and then opened his door and stepped out. He grabbed the six foot length of rubber tubing he used for transferring fuel and started walking toward the tractor to find the gas tank. He tried but failed to keep from looking at the trailer itself with its art. A family sitting down to dinner. The paint was faded but he could see the bright and smiling face of the mother holding a roasted chicken, could see the indulgent father and the boy and girl looking hungry. Alford Meats. Making families smile since 1974.

He wondered if there was food in the back of the truck but dismissed the idea. He couldn't hear the refrigeration unit working, if the truck even had one. It was possible the truck had been abandoned here years ago anyway. The gas would be old but it would work. He made his way forward and found the tank. It was enormous, a hundred or maybe two hundred gallons in a long silverfish cylinder that seemed to be placed too close to the hitch. He found the cap and held his breath as he wiped grime from it. He sighed. Diesel fuel only. He dropped the hose onto the ground and stepped to the cab to see if anything else could be scavenged.

The roar reached him before the impact but it didn't give him a chance to avoid the attack. He was able to avoid resistance so the momentum carried him away, stumbling, from the infected man.

Woman.

He turned around and backed away as she approached. If she'd been the driver of the truck, she was about as stereotypical a female truck driver as they came. He could see through years of grime the remnants of a flannel shirt of some kind. It was stained, along with what was left of her jeans, with blood, some of it fresh. She roared again and started toward him and he realized he'd stupidly left his weapons in the car. There was no easy way to get them because the truck driver stood between Hal and the weapons. She was long dead if dead was an accurate description. Portions of her skull were visible along the side of her face and the sickly white of her jawbone stood in horrible contrast to the strangely intact gums and teeth and tongue.

She was beyond hope. He could see that. Already her eyes glinted with excitement, instinct for violence. He scanned for something, anything. Realistically, his only hope was evasion but it wasn't a false hope. Though the sick didn't really lose any of their physical speed, they lost a great deal of their dexterity, their reaction time. He dove to the ground and rolled beneath the truck. His aim was off and he felt a sickening and sharp burst of agony as something caught on his shirt and dug into his flesh before tearing away as he rolled over. He gained some time, though. The driver let out a gurgling scream and he kept rolling until he'd rolled through to the other side. He was on his feet and moving before the creature decided how to follow. He paused for only a moment before heading toward the rear of the trailer. Nine times out of ten, someone as far gone as the lady would eventually decide to run in the shortest route but the idea of crawling under the truck would be difficult for her to manage. Around the trailer would get him to the weapons while she probably still waited.

So, when she slammed into him, sending him sprawling over the sand abutment and rolling into the overgrown drainage ditch, it took a moment for him to understand what the hell had happened. He felt slickness on his face and retched as he lifted himself up and tried to understand the situation. He'd rolled into gore, rotting intestines or rotting meat or rotting something. He wiped his eyes with the back of his hand. Coyote. There was a partially eaten coyote carcass, probably the truck driver's dinner for the last few days. He retched again and then felt her again, this time wrapping her arms around him as she attacked. He rolled, primarily to get her beneath him rather than above, and then he lifted his upper body up and slammed it backward.

Of course, it was no use.

There was no pain. Or, at least, the pain was dulled so damned dramatically that there was no pain enough to shock a zombie—goddam, he hated that word—into letting go. He tried again, this time grabbing her wrists through the flannel and pulling them apart. That separated them, and he leapt up and stumbled a few feet away until he could jump over the abutment and back to the truck. He wanted to run for the car but at this point he wasn't certain he'd make it, certainly wouldn't be able to get to the weapons easily. What he needed, more than anything else, was a moment to breathe.

The cab.

He rushed to the passenger door and yanked. It was locked. He rushed around and yanked on the driver's door. It opened but as he tried to step up, he felt her arms on him again. He slammed outward with the door but it only made her slide down so she gripped his legs and he ended up holding onto the seat belt to keep from falling. These situations always left him with a curious sense of conflict. The woman was clearly beyond hope, beyond any help he could offer her. Still, he couldn't bear to think of her as anything other than a woman, as a woman who once had hopes and dreams and perhaps still did. How could he? If she were beyond hope than wasn't it just inevitable that Lori and Kaylee would be beyond hope soon?

Kaylee. Lori. Ultimately, the need to protect them overcame his hesitance and though he winced as he did it, he lifted his free leg and brought it down hard on the truck driver's shoulder. The woman grunted but didn't stop.

Woman.

Creature.

Thing.

He tried desperately to consider her a thing as he pulled his foot back and brought it down again, this time on her face. He got a gurgled scream from her but her hands still didn't relax their grip on his leg. If anything, her grip tightened and Hal felt something visceral and realized it was real fear. It was urgent fear, fear he'd lost some time ago in the omnipresent state of continual, frightened despair. He cursed himself for leaving his weapons in the car, cursed himself for an oversight that would surely kill him and more importantly leave Lori and Kaylee unprotected. He kicked her again but again it did nothing to loosen her grip. In fact, she screamed and yanked hard and he found his own grip failing and slid down the seat belt strap so that she was able to throw her arms around his waist.

Then he saw it. He cursed himself because he should have known it would be there. Didn't most truckers keep them? The butt was about a foot away but it was risky because to reach it he'd have to let go of the strap with at least one of his hands. Hell, the damned thing might not be loaded and all he'd have would be a club. He had to risk it, though, and he shouted to give himself some energy as he let go with one hand and grabbed for the gun. His hand closed around the stock beneath the trigger, and the truck driver finally won the tug of war so both of them fell backward. The gun came out with them but he couldn't keep a grip on it, and it tumbled to the left while he and the woman tumbled to the right. She lost her grip momentarily with the impact of the fall and he scrambled away but she grabbed his leg again before he could get clear.

The gun—he could see it was a shotgun now—was about three feet past his outstretched hands, and he clawed at the ground to try to close the distance. He made about six or seven inches of progress but she yanked him backward so he lost it again. He rolled over and a rock on the shoulder of the road bit into the small of his back so that he screamed as sharp pain shot through him. It angered him, and fueled by the anger he kicked out again with his free leg, catching the driver on her chin, a solid kick that sent her sprawling back. Of course, she leapt for him again but he'd gained the time he needed. When she landed on him, the shotgun was pointed at her. It ended up wedged against her midsection and he pulled the trigger.

And not a damned thing happened.

For a moment, nauseous fear gripped him. The damned thing hadn't been loaded after all but as the butt dug into his shoulder, he realized he'd never pumped the action, so he screamed again and grabbed the pump with his free hand, pulling it down and hearing a satisfying click. He still didn't know if it was loaded but he pulled the trigger. The explosion left him hurt and deaf. In the struggle, the butt of the gun had moved to his chest, and he felt like something broke from the recoil. The driver, though, flew back and landed on the ground, her midsection more like shredded rags of flesh than a body. She was screaming, Hal thought, but the sound of the gun still rang in his ears so he couldn't be sure. He got to his knees, and the movement sent shards of hurt from his chest. Bruised ribs maybe but broken ribs probably. He still had to deal with her.

Head shots always killed them. They weren't the only things that killed them but they always did the trick. He could feel a tear running down his cheek as he lifted the gun to his shoulder again. He aimed for her head and hesitated because he knew the recoil would hurt like hell. Finally, the sight of her screaming face was too much and he whispered, "I'm sorry," and pulled the trigger. The sound was distant but the pain in his side was profound, and he saw the woman's face disappear in red mist as the edges of his vision blackened. He felt the ground beneath him leap up and then felt hands on his cheeks.

He opened his eyes.

It was night. He'd been out for at least three hours. Lori held his face in her hands.

***

He watched the fire as it flickered, sending interesting shadows against the truck. It took a great deal of time but he learned from Lori he'd been out for an entire day. She'd managed, with Kaylee's help, to drive the car behind the truck. That, in and of itself was remarkable. She'd grazed the driver's side against the trailer so there was a wide gash but appearance didn't really matter anymore. She'd left him on the ground, afraid to move him, but she and Kaylee had scavenged the truck. She'd put everything she thought might be of use in a little pile. There was a first aid kit, flares, and some blankets. There were also cigarettes, and Hal smoked one now. None of the food in the trailer was good except for a case of teriyaki beef jerky. A few packages of it was boiling along with a few onions and some canned corn over the fire.

There was something both frightening and reassuring about her actions. He was pretty sure she wouldn't have been able to keep things together if he'd been dead. On the other hand, he wasn't entirely certain she knew he'd wake up. Still, she hadn't reacted with blind instinct. She'd reacted, against all odds, as the Lori before all the shit hit the fan. She'd reacted, and she and Kaylee weren't wandering the desert or declining. Kaylee slept in the car at the moment but she sat beside him, and Hal looked at her in wonder. "You did good, Lori," he said.

"Well," she said. It took a long time to get out, and he looked at her expectantly. She stared back at him and said, "Well." He waited. "Not." He still watched her, trying his best not to become impatient. "Good," she said.

It took him a moment, and then tears welled up in his eyes. Well, not good. She'd corrected his grammar. She'd corrected his grammar! He reached for her and pulled her close to him, and before he could think about it, his mouth found hers.

Six months, really closer to three quarters of a year. He felt like weeping the entire time but he didn't, and she hadn't lost any of her skill even if she'd lost some of the speed. It was slow, sweet. When he finished, he lay atop her and felt the warmth of the fire against his sides and kissed her and finally wept. She slid her hand slowly up his back until she found his head and she stroked his hair softly and kissed his neck and his cheek.

They woke in the morning and his chest felt better but Lori insisted, in her way, that they address the injury so he used a roll of cloth sports bandages to wrap his ribs tightly. When he was finished, they woke Kaylee and ate jerky stew for breakfast. Kaylee played quietly at the side of the truck as they packed the car, and when he closed the trunk, Lori said, "Thought...you...didn't...want...me...anymore." He felt tears threatening and pulled her to him.

"More than I ever have, Lori." He fought back the tears. "More than I ever have."

He held her until she let go of him and called to Kaylee. He found it interesting that the two of them had no trouble finishing each others sentences or more commonly simply reacting to what the other was attempting to say. Kaylee made her way over, and for a moment Hal didn't recognize the feeling he felt. It was hope.

He secured them in the car and turned the engine over. He backed up and saw a car in the distance behind them. "Get down," he said. They obeyed but he felt a horrible sense of foreboding anyway, and he realized the car was slowing down. "In the glove box, Lori," he whispered. He kept his eyes focused on the rear view mirror and waited until Lori pressed the gun into his hand. The car was slowing, only about twenty yards back. The headlights filled the car and he lifted up his hand to make sure they could see the gun in it.

The car slowed and then pulled up beside them. The man in the driver's seat appeared to be alone. He was Hal's age. Maybe a little older. A lot more sedentary. Probably an accountant or a middle manager before the shit hit the fan. He too held a gun. Hal pressed the button on his door to bring the window down and the man did the same with his passenger window. "I don't want any trouble," the man said. Hal didn't reply and the man said, "Any food left in the truck."

Something about the man's eyes seemed vaguely familiar. It wasn't just the fear because the fear was on everyone's face these days. There was furtiveness. He hid something. Hal brought his gun down but only so he could chamber a round discretely as he said, "No. Well, yes. There was only some beef jerky, a case of it. We only kept about half, and the rest is around the side of the trailer."

The man nodded. "Thank you. I'll drive around. I don't want trouble."

We. God damn it. *We only kept about half.* That was an inexcusable mistake but the man didn't seem to notice. He nodded again and moved his car forward and Hal sighed in relief but then saw movement in the man's backseat and lifted his gun. He thought for a moment he caught a glint of metal but then dropped his gun. It wasn't silvery or even reflected tail lights. The glint was pink. The infected ducked back down but the glint was pink. Hal realized he was shaking as the man pulled in front of the truck and turned his engine off.

Hal turned his engine off, too, took a deep breath and stepped from the car.

"Please!" the man said. "I don't want any trouble." Hal looked at the man. He stood with his gun pointed toward them but his stance was all wrong. He didn't know how to use it.

Hal lifted his hands up and said, "I'm not going to hurt you. I don't want trouble either. I just want to show you something. Please, put down the gun and come over here."

"You want me to get rid of my gun."

"No," Hal said. "You can bring it. Just stop pointing at me." The man seemed like he was lost for a moment and Hal added, "We can help each other, maybe. Please. I won't hurt you and I won't hurt whoever's in the car." It was the wrong thing to say, and the man's eyes grew wide. He shook more and Hal worried that the gun would go off whether or not the man intended it.

"Lori," Hal said. "There's someone else, someone else like you and Kaylee. Sit up."

The man's expression didn't change and Hal realized his headlights likely made it hard for the man to see. "I'm going to turn off my lights," he said.

"Don't you move!"

"I'm going to turn out my lights so you can—"

"I said don't you move! I swear to God I'll shoot you and—" The man suddenly stopped speaking and his face seemed strange for a moment, almost crumpling. His hands seemed to grow weak and Hal watched as the gun fell from them and tears welled in the man's eyes.

"My God," the man said and Hal turned to follow his gaze. Lori stood there, out of the car, pink pupils almost glowing.

***

Frank. That was what the man claimed his name was but Hal was pretty sure it was something else because he didn't respond to Frank naturally but paused as though remembering his alias whenever he was addressed. His wife was Clara, and she reacted with only the typical slowness of the infected, so Hal was pretty sure that was accurate. They hadn't stayed at the truck. It was too likely anyone passing by would stop there. Instead, they drove with Frank behind and Hal in front for about four hours until they found a private house. It was probably a farm house before, and Hal led the tiny convoy down the private road to the location. More accurately, they drove down the private road down six empty stockyards and through several hills until Frank caught a glimpse of something that appeared to be a chimney and turned to investigate. The house lay in a small valley. Of course, the house was abandoned. However, Hal found goats grazing in the backyard, shot one, and thanked God for 4H years before as he butchered it. He brought the meat inside and discovered the stove still worked, which meant the place ran on propane and not municipal gas. He set the meat to simmering and then went out back again to shoot two more goats.

Frank approached him while he was skinning them. "We can't stay together for very long," Hal said. "You make it riskier for me and I make it riskier for you. But, these goats will give us each some meat for a day or so."

"Where are you going?"

"Away." He didn't mean it as a deflection. It was the only answer he had.

"I... I heard there was somewhere we could go." The man paused. So did Hal. He looked at Frank and raised an eyebrow. "I heard there's a hospital from when it first happened, and there are still doctors there and, well, they're just past the border."

"Mexico?"

"No, Canada."

"Quebec?" The French separatists in Quebec had finally gotten their wish while the world was falling down around them. They were a separate entity. Of course, most of Canada was anarchy now. The U.S. had fallen into a structure almost like city states. Canada had done the same but not giant cities like Toronto but an endless sea of smaller settlements.

"No. What used to be British Columbia, I think. It might be on our side of the border, though."

Hal sighed. "How do you know it's not just a goose chase?"

Frank shook his head. "I don't. It probably is but what the hell else am I supposed to do?"

"I don't think we can go there together. Washington and Oregon were hit hard but they're all survivalists there, the only hope of getting through there is by being less, not more, obvious."

Frank looked hopeless, and Hal felt horrible but he added, "This is too cliché anyway. Here we are in the end of the world but there's some city of refuge our heroes can escape to? That's every goddam apocalypse movie ever made."

Surprisingly, Frank didn't back down. "Maybe you're right. Maybe it is cliché. But that might be why there's a shot. Maybe someone thought about it, set it up."

Hal sighed. "I don't think there's any hope for it but even having a destination has got to be better than what we have going on now." He was pretty sure he wouldn't be heading that direction, pretty sure Frank wasn't careful enough. The best solution was to find somewhere in the mountains, far enough from civilization that they could live without fear of discovery, somewhere with game and fresh water. Sure, the family would live like they were settlers in the 1800s but he was pretty sure they could live a fine life there until some scientist somewhere discovered a cure.

He'd been raised on a small farm, and he'd hunted year round, his father not particularly concerned with the seasons and their farm remote enough that it didn't matter. Somewhere along the way they'd procure more ammunition and some livestock, maybe some seed to get started. It would be a hard life but it would be a good life. It would be a hell of a lot better than life as it was now. He didn't want the confrontation now. Already, Frank seemed too needy. They'd develop two routes to the supposed hospital in Canada and then Hal just wouldn't show up. It was the best course of action.

Best course of action.

He felt oppressive guilt pushing down on him. Jesus. Best course of action? He looked at Frank and then stood up. "We should stick together," he said. Frank looked surprised. "It's riskier in a lot of ways but neither of us have as much of a chance alone." He paused and then added. "I don't think there's a hospital but we can find somewhere, pick up supplies along the way and start a life somewhere. We'll head that direction but let's not tell them we're heading toward a cure."

"They don't deserve hope?"

The words hurt. Hal sighed and said, "They deserve hope, hope for what's possible." He started to walk away but instead sat back down. "But they don't deserve to be disappointed again when it doesn't happen."

Frank looked like he was going to reply but then his wife stepped onto the backyard carrying a bottle. It took a moment to see what it was. Whiskey, Irish whiskey. Hal raised an eyebrow. Clearly, at the end of the world, the most important issues were food, shelter, and water. Nevertheless, he hadn't found it all that surprising that the first thing that disappeared with all the looting was the booze. The beer and wine followed shortly thereafter. You could run across a bottle of beer or wine now and again but it was all but unheard of to find the good stuff. Sure, people made homemade brews and there was always shine available but it wasn't grain based and was risky and likely laced.

Lori followed Frank's wife, and she held two cups in her hands. She handed them to Frank. Frank's wife had to adjust her plans so it took her a moment to change course and hand the bottle to Hal. He thanked her and realized he didn't know her name. "Frank," he said. "My wife's name is Lori. My daughter is Kaylee."

Frank said, "She's not my wife. I mean, she is but we never made it official. I call her my wife and she calls me her husband but I had a modest inheritance, a trust fund back in college. We would have lost the income if I were married. So... well, we never got around to making it official even though it's been... God. Why the hell didn't I just take her to the courthouse and..."

His voice trailed off and Hal took a breath. "Things aren't over, Frank. You can still marry her."

Hal watched Clara bend over toward Frank. Clara, damn it. Her name was Clara. "Clara." The woman slowly pulled away from Frank and Hal said, "I remember your name now."

It took a while for her to smile but she did. Then, she tried to speak. Hal was patient but Frank seemed embarrassed. He started to say something but Hal held up a hand. "I read somewhere that when someone stutters or has a stroke you can't finish for them. I know this isn't the same thing but maybe it feels the same way for Clara." Frank nodded and Hal quickly added, "Or for Lori or Kaylee."

Clara tried again and after an eternity got out the word *more*. Frank and Hal waited but she was done and she was smiling. Frank asked softly, "More what?"

Lori answered. "Bar," she said. "Whole bar." Hal thought she spoke more quickly than she had in a while and he smiled broadly. She smiled back. Clara smiled as well. They seemed proud about their discovery, and Hal wondered at a world thrown back a hundred years or more where nonetheless, the discovery of spirits was a fabulous thing.

He smiled at the two of them. "Do you two want to get glasses?" Lori looked surprised and he said, "I think it will be fine. No interactions with the drugs and alcohol isn't going to spread any infection." He smiled again. "Just one glass, though." Lori took Clara's hand. He watched them slowly walk away and found it strange they could move with excitement but still move so slowly.

"You think it's an infection, then?"

Hal shrugged. "I think I want my wife to feel normal." He finished skinning the second goat and said, "Can you see if there's a shovel or something? We should bury the skins and the entrails. Just in case there are any of them around."

Frank nodded and stood. By the time he returned, the wives were back with glasses. Hal stood and said, "Frank and I need to clean up. How about you pour the drinks." He purposely didn't open the bottle and took Frank a short distance away, dragging the skins and the entrails atop them with him. Frank dug and Hal said, "Lori likes to do things even if it takes a long time. I think she's getting faster, too."

"She's getting better?"

Hal nodded. "Yeah, I think so. Use it or lose it, maybe."

***

By the time they finished with the two new skins and the one from earlier, the women had glasses full and waiting. Everyone also had a plate of stewed goat and Kaylee ate inside. Hal sat next to Lori and kissed her cheek. Frank seemed surprised but he leaned over and kissed Clara as well. Hal saw movement and panic welled up for a moment but it was Kaylee, stepping closer and then making her slow way to Hal and Lori. He kissed her cheek as well and said, "It's time for bed, little one." She groaned but then simply lay at his feet and closed her eyes. He smiled and shrugged and then took a sip of his whiskey.

Heaven.

Jesus. How long had it been? He drank bourbon, sometimes Tennessee, but he didn't like Irish whiskey. It just didn't go down as smoothly as bourbon. Hate was probably too strong a term but he'd skipped the hard stuff altogether if his preference wasn't available.

But it tasted like Heaven nonetheless. It burned nicely going down and he savored it but then noticed the carcasses of the goats on the porch. "We'll have to limit it to one drink until we can get those processed. I think we might have to smoke them."

Lori touched his hand and he turned his head. She took a long time to form words but she finally managed to say, "RV."

Hal nodded and said, "We don't have it anymore, Honey. We..." He trailed off because he was almost... it sure as hell seemed like she rolled her eyes. She smiled a half smile, a smile closer to one of her sardonic smiles from before. He suddenly wanted her again and he breathed in sharply. He fought back the emotions, though, and said. "Here. You mean there's an RV here." She nodded slowly. "Where?"

She shrugged. It took a long time to figure out exactly what expression she tried to make but she shrugged. "Did you see an RV?" Hal asked.

Her response came slowly but she said, "Clara."

Frank turned to Clara. "Did you see an RV?"

Clara shook her head slowly and then said, "Come, follow...Nathan."

Nathan. Frank was Nathan. Hal smiled but didn't say anything. Frank looked ashamed and then said, "Nathan is my middle name. What did she mean?"

Hal said, "Ask her. She's still Clara, Nathan."

He turned to his wife. "What do you mean?"

Clara stood and motioned for him to follow. Frank stood and so did Hal. Lori smiled and said, "Kaylee." She didn't stand. Hal nodded and kissed her cheek. Clara turned around and began her slow walk back into the house. She led them through the kitchen and into a small adjoining room. The adjoining room had the bar, a beautiful oak bar someone sank a great deal of money into. He paused and looked behind it. Mostly glassware but five more bottles of Irish whiskey were in an open box. He saw a few mixers, a bottle of gin, and a half-open bottle of vodka.

He put the gin in the empty slot in the case of whiskey and lifted it to the top of the bar. Lori stared disapprovingly at him, and he was almost too shocked by her ability to create the expression to protest. "Alcohol is antiseptic," he said. "We may drink a little bit for special occasions but this is for medicine." He was almost certain she rolled her eyes again but she did it with a smile. He sighed. "Clara, please show me the RV."

He followed slowly behind the women as Clara walked to a door, opened it, and then stepped out of the way. She took a great deal of time to gesture for him to look inside but he waited patiently. Lori was very far advanced compared to Clara. Perhaps Clara was simply advanced in the disease. He didn't know. He nodded to her and stepped inside the room.

It was a pantry, and it was remarkable because the pantry was full. There were canned goods as well as pasta and beans in canisters embossed with roses and grapes. There was even hot chocolate in a tin, and he wondered why nobody had looted the house. In fact, the house seemed pretty damned intact altogether, and that made no sense at all. He turned back to Clara and said, "This is good, really good. Why did you say RV, though?"

She lifted her hand and Hal realized she was pointing. He'd grown accustomed to waiting for Lori or Kaylee to finish their words and gestures so the impatience that hit him suddenly was unexpected. He held on even though he had to clench his teeth to do so and when she stopped moving her hand he looked where she pointed. On the top shelf were RV supplies. There were cans of toilet treatment, rolls of tissue designed for portable toilets, and a few other odds and ends. There were also batteries, large batteries he assumed handled the RV auxiliary power. Clara hadn't seen an RV. She'd seen evidence of one. That was inductive reasoning. That was remarkable.

He turned. "This is a great discovery. The RV might be here and we'll have to search the property. On the other hand, the people who lived here might have been traveling when... well, when everything happened." Both women nodded and he made it official. Lori only took about two-thirds of the time to complete the affirmation as Clara took. He smiled and said, "Why don't we finish our drinks and in the morning we can try to find the RV?"

She nodded, and Hal thought perhaps she nodded more quickly than she had before.

***

He made love to Lori again, this time in a king sized bed under dusty blankets but blankets still. He felt normal, and though he thought perhaps it was better because they'd broken the ice by the truck he suspected it was more than that. She was better. She'd been awkward before, physically awkward. She didn't move like some kind of porn star now but she moved a hell of a lot faster than she had before. By the truck, she was like a virgin experiencing things for the first awkward time. Now, she was like a 1970s European soft core actress, moving slowly and gently but still actively participating. He held tightly to her afterward and then rolled over and she put one leg over him and her head on his shoulder.

Like before.

Like before everything.

He stroked her back and realized she was crying softly. He lifted her head and kissed her. "We're going to get through this," he said. "We will." She kissed him, on his mouth, and though it still took a while, she told him she loved him.

She rolled off and though she was slow, she was still faster than before. He was certain of it. He watched her walk to the walk-in closet and open it. Kaylee lay there sleeping. Was it activity that did it? Was it like physical therapy? Maybe they could never get rid of the pink eyes but was it really something as simple as using it or losing it? He chuckled softly and Lori turned to look at him. He didn't tell her he was considering marathon sex sessions as treatment. Instead, he told her he loved her and he was happy and that someday they would find a house like this where they could try to be normal. She smiled and came back to bed.

In the morning, he was surprised to find Clara up and excited. Frank/Nathan was still asleep. Lori walked to Clara and hugged her, and Hal wondered if there was some kind of secret language the two shared. Did all of the infected share a language? He wondered why they didn't attack each other, the ones who were far gone with the condition. He'd always assumed there was something in the disease, some pheromone or something. With the way the two interacted, though, he thought perhaps there was more. Finally, Lori let go and walked to Hank. Her expressions were definitely clearer. Were they? Was he too hopeful?

She kissed him and said, "She found it." He waited but that was it. She'd said the words and there was almost no delay. She seemed like she was on the brink of laughing at his shocked expression and she kissed him again. Her second sentence took much longer to get out. "Hurry before her boss wakes up."

He nodded and started toward Clara but then stopped. "Boss?"

Clara looked a little embarrassed but from behind him, Lori giggled and it actually almost sounded like a giggle. He turned to look at her and the smile that greeted him was almost mischievous.

***

The RV was a class C. They'd rented one every summer before Kaylee and then one week a year. This was a newer model. It was in something that looked like a barn, and it was hooked up, still plugged in and still connected to the sewer drain. Hal tried the driver's door. It worked. The keys hung from the visor. He recognized the ignition keys but he also recognized the keys to all of the compartments along the side as well as the side door. He grabbed them and walked around. The side door was unlocked so he didn't have to use the key. When he opened the door, a step slid out with an electric whirring sound. There was still power. He stepped inside. The thing was clean. Perfectly clean.

Except for the dust.

There weren't any cobwebs but he could smell cedar and mothballs. He imagined the owners were in their fifties before everything fell apart. He imagined the husband was an engineer or something, someone who worked off checklists. Even the dust wasn't that bad. He surveyed things. The stove was propane rather than electric. That was good. There was a bunk above the cab. A couch. It became a bed. The dining area sat four or five and it collapsed into a bed as well. He walked past the refrigerator and saw the shower and the bathroom. Good working order, it appeared. He opened the door beyond them and stared in at the master room. Again, it was very well kept. Only dust.

Hall walked back out and tested the engine. Worked. He went back outside and opened each compartment in turn. The RV was stocked will all of the RV essentials. Flares, tool kit, first aid kit, spare bulbs, spare fuses. He was particularly happy to find a solar switch right next to the propane tanks. He climbed underneath. The propane tank was detachable. That was good. It was still fairly common to come across standard propane tanks with gas. It was near to impossible to find anywhere to fill them. He climbed into the driver's seat and turned the key. He didn't know why he found it so surprising that the RV worked but it worked. He saw there were two tanks and saw the thing ran on diesel. That would actually make things easier. There were far more abandoned trucks than cars. The gauge showed a full tank. He flipped a switch above it and the gauge fell to two-thirds of a tank. Two tanks. Good to know.

He turned off the engine and said, "Your boss?"

Clara looked embarrassed again and Hal realized she was probably twenty years younger than Frank. "Are you safe with him?" She nodded her head vigorously or at least as vigorously as she could and Hal nodded. "Okay. We have some work to do. Why don't you two and Kaylee see about cleaning this up and then packing up the food and the supplies. He thought a moment and then said, "Hold on." He drove forward and out of the barn. He turned off the engine again and then climbed out. He walked several yards away and caught the glint of panels on the roof. He made his way back, opened the compartment, and toggled the switch that initiated the solar power. Then, he climbed back into the RV and held his breath as he reached for a light switch.

It worked.

He sat down on the couch and tried to figure out how to handle things. He sure as hell wasn't going to let Frank or Nathan or whatever the hell his name was drive the RV but that meant leaving his car behind and he wasn't inclined to give up his car. It was a stupid vanity, sure, but it was still there. He sighed and considered just taking Lori and Kaylee and leaving. He wanted to take Clara, too, imagined what it had to be like. The girl was probably in her very early twenties. She was probably eighteen or nineteen before she became infected, and that meant the asshole had been fucking a girl who was all but a child.

Jesus. Was he just keeping her around for the guaranteed lay?

He felt bile rising in his throat and leapt from the couch and out of the RV, retching horribly as he shot partially digested goat onto the grass. He stumbled farther away from the RV and that was when he saw the glint of metal against the side of the barn. He made his way over and then stopped a few yards away. There were two of them, obviously the owners of the RV. They screamed when they saw him and stretched their hands toward him but they were pinned down. Their throats had deteriorated enough that their screams were no more than raspy whispers.

He stepped closer. It was hard to see exactly what had fallen on them but it looked like machined steel. A closer look told him it was almost like part of the frame of a pre-fabricated steel building. They were four or five yards from the side of the barn. He looked up. There were more of the steel frames on the roof of the barn. He still couldn't see how it had worked to pin them but thought perhaps they'd climbed on the roof or something like that and fallen...no. It didn't make sense. They were too old to climb. More likely an animal climbed on the roof at the wrong moment and a poorly balanced stack shifted.

They were pinned opposite each other, and that made the situation even more tragic. Each had torn the flesh from the others legs. A goat skeleton lay next to the man as well. Hal sighed and reached for his gun.

Damn.

He made his way back toward the house and into the bedroom where he'd slept. He reached for the duffel bag but stopped when he saw movement. "I'm sorry," Frank/Nathan said. "But I'm taking the RV. I'm taking it with Clara." Hal turned his head slowly. The man had Hal's gun.

"Does Clara know about this?"

"Wake up. Clara doesn't know anything. None of them do." The man gestured with the gun. Hal wasn't sure if he knew how to use it but the man seemed comfortable with it in his hand. "We're with walking vegetables. That's it. They're good for pussy and nothing else." He paused and his smile almost made Hal sick again. "Good pussy, though. The best. They spread their legs when you tell them to and they don't argue with you afterward. You know, Clara was a huge problem before all this happened. Now she knows her place."

"Was she going to tell your wife, Frank?"

The man's eyes narrowed. Hal knew he'd hit a nerve but the man replied evenly. "Right now, you and your pets get to live. We'll take the RV and the supplies and we'll leave. You want to change that? You want me to put a bullet in your brain and have more than one pair of docile legs to spread whenever I want?"

His instinct was to leap up and attack but Hal fought down the urge. Then, he saw Clara in the doorway. He took a deep breath. "Don't you love Clara?"

The man laughed. "Love? That was all she wanted before this shit happened. Look, I loved the way she could move her body, I'll give you that. I loved that I could do anything, anything at all. If my wife didn't give it to me, Clara would. Sure, she's more like some fucking plastic blow up doll now but that's better than nothing."

"Don't you give a damn about how she feels?"

"How she feels? Grow up. Jesus. Listen up, Boy Scout. I really care about how she feels when I'm screwing her. How's that?" Clara's eyes were sad, not quite filled with tears but sad. Hal watched her step away and to cover the noise he stood up. Immediately, Frank trained the gun on him and said, "What the hell do you think you're doing?"

Hal lifted his hands. "I want to go downstairs and get you keys so you can leave." He wanted to add how much Frank sickened him but he didn't. "Unless you want to try them yourself," he said.

Frank eyed him narrowly and said, "Okay. Let's go." Hal walked carefully past him and out of the bedroom. The man walked behind him, making his steps obvious, making sure Hal knew he was there.

"Is it Frank or is it Nathan?"

"What?"

"Your real name. Which is it?"

"Why the hell does that matter anymore?"

Hal shrugged. It didn't matter, not really. "Were you in love with your wife before this happened?"

"You talk too much."

"What if they can still think? What if they can still feel?" It was a pretty damned stupid question, really. The man didn't give a damn about her thoughts and her feelings before.

"Have you ever had an affair?"

"No."

There was a pause. They were near the door to the backyard now, and Hal could almost see the expression on Frank's face in the glass door. It was indecision. "You know," Hal began but the man interrupted him.

"When you're married your wife has expectations all the time. Then some beautiful young girl shows up at your office and she adores you, she wants you without all those expectations. You don't have to prove anything to her. You don't have to be anything than older and her boss for her to love everything about you."

Hal reached the door. "It's not too late to give her a real reason to love you."

"Just get the keys, and don't try anything."

Hal slid the door open and stepped out. He walked to the RV, moving slowly in the hopes a brilliant plan would spring to mind but nothing came. He could take Frank, Nathan. He could take whatever the hell his name was but he wasn't sure he could do it without a wound and he wasn't confident he could keep that wound from pushing him into sepsis. "Listen. This is a bad choice—"

"Just shut up! This is happening and you can either live with it or die right here."

He sighed again and made walked to the driver side door. He opened it and pulled down the visor. The keys were gone. "You already took the keys?"

"What? What the hell are you talking about?"

He turned to face him. "What kind of game are you playing? The keys are already gone."

Frank looked nervous, frightened. "I may not be the kind of guy who stars in blockbusters but I have the goddam gun and I'll use it." Hal wasn't certain if he'd really use it but he was certain the man had no morality left.

"I don't have them. They're gone."

"I will kill your daughter and then your—"

"Hid... them..." Hal turned to see Clara. She had her arm up and pointed at Hal. She repeated the words and an eternity passed as she did. Lori and Kaylee stood next to her, looking scared.

Frank/Nathan smiled and walked toward them. "You're going to tell me where you hid the damned keys or you can just say goodbye to one of them. Which one Hal? You want to say goodbye to your already dead wife or your already dead daughter?" He shouted the last words and raised the gun. Hal prepared to leap toward him as his heart raced but Clara stepped in front of her ex-boss.

"You...don't...love...me?"

Frank lifted up his hands. "Of course I do," he said sweetly. "I'm doing all of this for you."

"Heard... talk... him."

"Darling," he said. "Anything you heard I only said because he's dangerous. That's why I need the keys, to get away from him." He lifted his arm and pointed the gun at Kaylee. "You have three seconds, Hal." Hal prepared to attack but Clara put her hand on Frank's wrist.

"I... know... hid... them..."

Frank smiled and the smile grew malicious as he turned to Hal and said, "See. She knows her place." He gestured with the gun and Hal followed the direction until he stood next to Lori and Kaylee. Frank turned his attention back to Clara. "Where did you see him hide them?"

"No... I... hid..."

Something was wrong. Hal didn't know what it was but Lori wasn't afraid. She was sad. He was pretty sure she was sad. It was possible he misinterpreted her expression but he didn't think so. He'd seen that expression time and time again. Lori wasn't afraid.

Kaylee was.

Kaylee was afraid. She held tightly to Lori's hand and stared at her father expectantly. She expected something from him, something miraculous. Hal wondered for a moment why he still found it so difficult to accept his daughter's disappointment, even now when life itself was nothing but disappointment. He sighed and said, "You can still stop this, Frank."

"You don't know anything," the man said. "My name isn't Nathan or Frank. That was my company."

"Frank and Nathan's? The video stores?" Hal tried to remember the press releases. The places would be out of business but they kept their adult choices long after the larger chains bowed to pressure. Then, abruptly, the firm announced some kind of accounting problems. Hal shook his head. "The infection was the only thing that kept you out of prison."

"Like this isn't prison?" The man's eyes narrowed. "Now give me the keys."

"I don't know where they are."

"I... know..."

The man nodded. "Get something to tie him to the RV." Clara looked around in confusion and the man snapped, "Rope damn it. Get some God damned rope or something." The girl jumped (as much as someone in her condition could) and then went to the RV, opening one of the side compartments and rummaging around. That just didn't make sense.

Didn't make sense?

That was bullshit.

She wouldn't have thought to look there. What the hell was going on? He turned to look at Clara but couldn't see anything of note. He turned to look at Lori. She still looked sad but there was definitely no fear. Clara stood up.

Christ.

She had a gun, a shotgun. It wasn't one of Hal's, and Hal hadn't seen it with Frank/Nathan's things. It wasn't too surprising that there'd be a gun on property in this part of the country or really in any part of the country in a home so secluded but it was surprising Clara found it instead of Hal.

"Not…" Clara began as she pointed the gun at Frank/Nathan. "Not…"

"Steal," Lori said.

Clara nodded slowly. "Yes. Not steal RV."

Frank looked incredulous and Hal understood. Were they getting better or were they always better? Were their minds just stiff, needing stretching? It was impossible. None of it made sense.

Except the guns.

They made far too much sense.

Frank/Nathan's face remained incredulous for a moment and Hal looked back at Clara. He doubted she'd ever used a gun in real life. He knew Lori hadn't. The shotgun was a pump shotgun and from the state of the RV, Hal doubted the man who'd owned it was the type to leave a shell in the chamber. He looked back at Frank and watched his face grow angry. The man trained the gun on Clara, murder evident in his expression.

"Wait," Hal said softly. "I know where the keys are."

"No!" He turned to look at Lori. She hadn't managed that level of intensity in her voice for a very long time.

"Where are they?"

"I'll show you," Hal said.

He wasn't certain what the hell he was going. All he knew for certain was that if the situation remained as it was Frank would fire and it was likely Clara would die. It might be too much of a stretch for Frank to accept that Lori and Clara had collaborated on the little insurrection but the risk was too high. He had to get the man to follow him and somehow find an opportunity to get the gun away from him.

He'd have to kill him.

Hal felt horrible about it but there wasn't any choice. He had to kill him. The man would always be a threat and he'd be a greater threat in close quarters. He turned to Clara. "Lower the gun, Clara."

"No." He thought for a moment her eyes glinted with tears.

"Please, Clara," he said. "It will be okay. We'll all be okay." It seemed to take forever but the barrel of the shotgun finally came down.

"Show me," Frank said. Hal walked around the front of the RV with no real idea where he planned to go and caught movement in the distance. He paused and stared. There were dozens of them. Maybe tens of dozens. "What the hell are those?" Frank asked.

"Goats," Hal said.

"Then why the hell is there grass? That many goats would have decimated this place. It should be dirt."

Hal shrugged. It was a good question. There was no reason for the goats to leave... Hal sighed. "The keys are this way," he said as he walked into the grass and then turned toward the barn. He walked and counted the steps. Frank spoke about five steps sooner than he'd expected him to.

"Wait!" Hal stopped and turned. Frank looked at him narrowly. "You think you're so damned smart, don't you. You have a gun stashed? Hung the keys up next to keys? You want the harem to yourself, you asshole?"

Hall shook his head sadly. "There's no gun."

"Bullshit. Where are the keys?" Hal sighed, shook his head sadly one more time, turned and pointed. Frank smirked slightly and said, "Okay. You move toward the left for me. I'm going to walk ahead but this gun will be on you the whole time. Don't get any ideas or I won't just take the damned RV. I'll put a god damned bullet in your head and leave you right where it's parked."

Hal didn't reply. He sighed and stepped to the left and then watched as the man stepped next to him, moving at a slight angle so the gun remained trained on Hal's body. Now was the time. A quick strike with his leg to the knee would incapacitate him, and if he got a shot off it would go wide, very wide. Nothing about the man was physically imposing. A quick kick and a quick follow up with his fist would incapacitate him, eliminate the threat, and diffuse the entire situation. The kick would take less than a second.

He didn't kick him. Instead, he walked along sadly. "There's still time to stop all this," he said softly. Frank stopped and turned fully toward him. There was just a little bit of uncertainty in his eyes. That was enough. A quick fist to his throat would incapacitate him with no real damage. A simple motion, really. A step forward, putting his weight on his right leg and a straight jab to ensure he hit the throat and not the side of the next. Frank would probably drop the gun but it wouldn't matter if he didn't. He'd be useless. He'd be utterly useless.

Hal desperately wanted to jab at his throat. All morality suggested he should but he didn't. Frank walked backward, the gun trained on Hal and he scowled. "You'd like that, right? We all go our merry way and I spend every second wondering when you're going to shoot me in the back of the head. That's what this is all about, you just waiting for the chance. You're lucky I don't just kill you. It's mercy to let you live. You'd never do it for me." Hal stopped moving. Frank stopped as well but then smiled. "Don't you dare try anything." He kept the gun trained on Hal before he turned around.

Before he turned around and screamed.

Before he turned around and the female put her teeth into his calf and tore a chunk of it out. The gun fell to the ground and bounced slightly. Hal felt a wave of guilt as Frank lunged for it, succeeding only in falling to the ground and making it possible for the male to get to his arm as the man screamed and flailed about impotently. Frank screamed primal screams, wordless screams.

Panicked screams.

Hal might have been able to save him before the male got involved. He couldn't now. He couldn't even offer him a release from the pain. The gun was too close to the two infected. He wanted to shoot him, to give him that mercy but the gun was too close. He stared, though he desperately wanted to look away. He stared and considered it penance that he should watch a man eaten alive, a man murdered by Hal.

Murder?

Self-defense?

There was no rationalizing it, as much as he wanted to. He'd consciously decided to kill him, consciously decided to do so with the husband and wife zombies who themselves deserved the mercy of permanent darkness. He looked at Frank. The man beat at the male eating his arm but he couldn't have much strength left. Anything he gained from adrenaline was counteracted by the loss of blood. Already, the woman had a large portion of his calf stripped from the bone so that sickly white mingled with the red and black gore.

He could chance the gun. He could move in, grab it, back off, and put a bullet in Frank's head. Perhaps that would be the only thing that allowed him to sleep soundly ever again. It was too close. The male might be distracted by his meal but Hal couldn't risk it. If he were killed, or even hurt, the chances for Lori and Kaylee grew slight and that wasn't acceptable. There was no choice but to—

His ears seemed to explode with pain as he watched Frank's head disappear into red vapor. He turned, a little deaf, and saw Clara holding the shotgun. He wasn't certain if he'd ever experienced such profound gratitude and profound guilt at the same time. Surprise, too. She'd known how to chamber a round, perhaps even how to load the gun. Frank didn't scream anymore but the meal continued and he held out his hand. Clara seemed relieved to give him the weapon. He trained it on the male and then the female, awarding peace to the two of them but still leaving images in his head he knew would linger. He looked at Clara. Her expression was unreadable.

"Sorry," she said. Hal didn't know if she said it to apologize to him or to Frank.

"I'll bury him," he said.

She nodded and said, "Them... too."

"Yes," he said. "Can you, can you go back to the RV? Can you make sure Lori and Kaylee know you're fine, know I'm fine?" She nodded again and seemed grateful for a purpose as she walked away. Hal leaned against the side of the barn and slowly slid to a seated position, holding his head in his hands.

***

"Why don't we stay?" It was early, and Hal opened his eyes to see Lori staring back at him. She seemed normal again, normal but for the pink pupils. She seemed normal and he was certain there'd been no hesitation in her voice.

"What did you say?"

"Why don't we stay?" He sat up and stared at her. The bodies were buried and buried deeply. He'd done it unnecessarily, really. He'd dug deep for his own benefit, to make the task somehow more meaningful, more profound. He hadn't done it to keep the bodies from attracting other infected but it would have the same effect nonetheless. He'd finished and somehow leaving didn't make sense and they all ended up remaining for one more night.

One more.

"What if he was right, Lori?" he asked. "What if there's a place in Canada where they're trying to find a cure. What if there's a safe haven."

"He was a liar." Again, her voice came so naturally, so perfectly that he felt a flood of sudden and desperate desire for her. He reached for her and pulled her to him, kissing her deeply. They made love, and this time without the almost overwhelming urgency they'd shared at the side of the road by the truck. Instead, he explored her slowly and wept when they finished so she held him and stroked his hair as he faded to sleep again. He awoke to the smell of coffee. He'd need to start rationing things.

He made his way down and to the kitchen. Lori sat at the table and smiled at him. "Why don't we stay?" she asked again as she got up and walked to the coffee pot. She poured him a mug and handed it to him. "Why don't we stay?"

He looked out the sliding glass window and saw Clara playing with Kaylee. Even happy, Kaylee always had a haunted look but it didn't seem to be there at the moment. Surely it was his eyes and not her expression but he didn't mind. "What if there's a haven out there?"

"Here is a haven."

He smiled but kept his eyes on Kaylee. "Is Clara okay?"

She didn't reply so he turned to look at her. "Here is a haven," she repeated.

It was secluded. There were goats that would last for some time, perpetually if he managed the stock and bred them. He could probably get a garden working. They could always leave later. They could keep the RV stocked and ready to go at a moment's notice. On the other hand, they could likely gather others to the place.

"Here is a haven," she said insistently.

"I suppose it is," he said. Lori reached over and put her hand over his, squeezing gently.

OUR LIVING FUNERAL

by Chelsey Baker

The heavy, beige colored subway doors closed with a definitive thud. Riley sat perfectly still in her seat, feeling the momentum of the train move her body as it slowly picked up speed again, careening down the track she couldn't see. Her green eyes wandered until she could see her mother's shoulders in her periphery, mere inches away from her own. Nancy had on a floral blouse with cut out shoulders. Riley could see her mother's tan skin slightly sway as the subway rushed forward under the Chicago streets. Since the divorce, Riley's mother had begun to dress like a woman half her age.

Nancy stared down at the grungy brown floor of the train. All she could see was a myriad of shoes and a piece of foil from a gum wrapper. She wiggled her feet, watching the overhead light shine off of her red toenails. Her eyes wandered to her daughter's shoes beside her. She wore dingy black Chuck Taylors. A hole had begun to form near one of the soles.

"You need new shoes," Nancy said quietly.

Riley glanced down at her feet. "These are fine," she replied.

"Fine? There's a hole in your right one."

Riley sighed, staring at the fake happy people that smiled down at her from the advertisements that lined the ceiling of the train car. There were so many things, a litany of things, she could argue with her mother about. Her shoes felt too easy as the subject.

"I'll get new ones, alright?" Riley said and scratched her cropped brown hair.

Nancy hated when Riley moved her arms about. She always tried to look away, but it felt as though her eyes were magnetic and couldn't help but stare at the crooks of her daughter's elbows. A series of red sores and bruises covered her daughter's pale, sallow looking skin. Most had scabbed over but they still looked angry, defiant almost. It felt as though each little sore looked back at Nancy, mocking her.

"You didn't have a long sleeved shirt to wear?"

Riley turned her neck to look at her mother. Her light brown eyes were steely as she gazed back. Fine lines surrounded the corners of Nancy's lips. Riley had the same slightly upturned nose as her mother, but it was the only thing that looked familiar. It was the only thing they shared.

"I'm sorry that my addiction embarrasses you," Riley snapped through gritted teeth.

She didn't bother to keep her voice down. An elderly man with thick round glasses glanced at her before blinking and turning his head away.

It had only been four hours since Riley had been kicked out of the Gateway Alcohol and Drug Treatment Center, but she absorbed her mother's shame as though it were her favorite sweater. It was familiar.

"I'm not embarrassed," Nancy snapped, running a hand through her shoulder length brown hair. "I just... Don't like to see what you've done to your body."

Silence reigned. Mother and daughter listened as the train clicked and whirred along the track. Their bodies swayed slightly as the subway shifted upward, barreling up from underground towards Belmont.

Riley watched as trees suddenly appeared on either side of the murky windows, brown and green blurs that lined the two story brownstones, built in rows along the track.

Her thoughts meandered to Gateway, and the way the woman at the front desk looked at her as she was being escorted out by security. She pictured the joint, all wrinkled and burnt, that her counselor had found in her room. It was just to take the edge off—the dive and plummet of withdrawal that had her body in a vice grip. But all they had seen was a rule broken.

Nancy sighed, feeling the subtle ache of a headache begin to form in the center of her forehead. Her thoughts were also on Gateway, and the conversation she had with Tim before she had driven to pick up her daughter.

"Jesus, she got kicked out again?" her ex-husband had complained on the phone. "How could you let this happen?"

She had hung up on him, but his words clung to the air around her like smoke. How could you let this happen? They were divorced and Riley's addiction to heroin still caused them to argue. It felt like their marriage had died the moment their daughter put a needle to her flesh.

Nancy rubbed her temples, glancing at the people around them. The man with the thick glasses that sat across from them had dozed off, his head tilted back against the wall. A heavy set woman with bushy blonde hair read a romance novel beside him. To the right was a middle aged Asian man frowning as he stared down at his phone.

A cough rang out. Nancy followed the sound to the other side of the train, where a balding man sat in the corner. His skin was pasty and slightly shiny with sweat. He sat hunched in a dark green jacket, gazing at the floor.

Nancy's stomach lurched and she forced herself to look away. The man looked how Riley did whenever she stopped using. Those days where her daughter shivered and said she was ready to be done with heroin for good. How many times had those words left her lips? How many times did Nancy have to endure hearing them, knowing they were false?

The train began to slow as it approached a stop. The dozing man opened his eyes, and got to his feet with a soft groan. The woman with the romance novel glanced up at him as she turned a page. The heavy subway doors slid open and the man trudged off. A young woman with a purple backpack walked onto the train, her tennis shoes squeaking slightly as she turned left and sat in an empty seat across from the coughing man.

The doors came to a close, and everyone leaned to the right as the train began to move. Riley felt her stomach drop slightly as the tracks began to dip down, hurling underground again. The train grew darker as it sunk into a tunnel.

The sickly looking man began to cough again, his body heaving with the effort. Nancy found herself unable to take her eyes off him. It wasn't just the germs he spread with his incessant coughing, there was something about his eyes that looked strange, though she couldn't quite put her finger on it.

As she watched him, the man slowly rose unsteadily to his feet. His eyes were dazed as he stared at the sticky brown floor of the L train. He opened his mouth and a low, almost guttural sound emanated from his pale lips.

"What the—" Riley began when the man suddenly turned to his right and lunged at the young woman with the purple backpack.

The woman stared up in horror as the man opened his mouth wide and bit into her neck with a sickening, sepulchral noise. He tore into her flesh. Nancy and Riley watched in horror and leapt from their seats, as the other train goers cried out and screamed. There were eight people total, including the sick man. All of them flew over seats and down the aisle way.

All but one.

The heavy set blonde woman trembled in her seat, her brown eyes wide with shock as she watched the sick man continue to devour the young woman. Her hazel eyes were turned toward the ceiling, but they could no longer see.

Riley and her mother stood with the others on the opposite side of the train. There were five of them total. The middle aged Asian man who had been on his phone clutched at his heart through his shirt, breathing heavily. A teenaged girl cried in the corner, her heavy black eyeliner ran down her face. Between the two was a muscular black man with a gold earring. Riley stared at the blonde woman, her fingers still clutching the pages of her romance novel in her seat.

"MOVE!" Riley bellowed.

Her voice was loud and frantic. The sick man looked up from the young woman's corpse, his face covered in her blood. His eyes, which seemed to have turned slightly yellow, shifted from Riley to the blonde lady. He growled, shoving the dead woman aside as though she were a rag doll, and stood upright. His gaze seemed hazy and unfocused. Nancy got the distinct impression that the man, whoever he was, was no longer fully there. His movements were clumsy, uncoordinated, and his expression was vacant. She wondered if he had lost all cognitive function.

The passengers on the train watched as the sick man charge forward just as the blonde woman did. She tossed herself from her seat, but her heavy body made her slow. The sick man squealed and jumped onto the woman's back.

She cried out as her legs buckled underneath his weight. Before her head hit the ground, he had already dug his teeth into the side of her neck. Blood gushed onto the floor of the train as he made contact with her carotid artery.

"No!" shrieked the teen, frantically shaking her head. Her dyed black hair flew about her face as she stared at the growing pool of blood on the floor.

"Quiet!" the black man snapped, glaring at her. "You'll attract its attention."

"Oh," Riley said and pushed between the two. Behind them was a metal door with a square window in the center. Below the window, in bold red letters read STOP DO NOT OPEN EMERGENCY USE ONLY.

Riley grabbed the silver handle and jerked it to the left, hearing the gears shift. She opened the door and waved at her mother and the others. "Into the next car!" she urged.

The Asian man was the first to run through, followed by the black man. He had grabbed the teenager's hand and pulled her after him. Nancy looked at her daughter with an appalled expression, then walked over the threshold.

The next car only had two people in it. One was a red haired man with clusters of freckles all over his face. He immediately stood up, watching as everyone piled in with a bemused expression. The other passenger was a middle aged woman with beautiful olive toned skin.

"What the hell is going on?" the red haired man demanded, looking at each of them.

"We don't know, this man just started attacking people!" the teenaged girl blubbered. She touched the metal spikes on her choker nervously.

"It's alright," the black man said, staring into their former car through the window. "The door is locked; he can't get to us."

Nancy stepped around the group and walked to the right wall of the train. Halfway up was a metal box that jutted out from the wall. On the left side was a speaker and a small silver button. "I'm gonna call the conductor," she said, and pressed the button down with her index finger.

"Hello?" Nancy said into the speaker. "There is an emergency! A man is attacking people! The police need to be called!"

Her request was met with a few moments of static and then nothing.

"Hello?!" she yelled. "Can anybody fucking hear me?!"

The teenager sobbed and sank into a seat. The Asian man sat beside her, blinking over and over again. Riley wondered if he was in shock.

"Is anybody getting service?" the black man asked, frowning down at the phone in his hand.

One by one each Chicagoan whipped out their phones and shook their heads. There were many sections of the L where nobody got service. They were underground, beneath several layers of metal and concrete.

"What do we do? What do we do?" the teenager asked, her pale, skinny body trembling.

"We should keep moving," the Asian man said, his voice soft but certain. "We should put as much distance between us and that man as humanly possible."

The black man shook his head, absentmindedly touching his moustache. "I disagree. I think we should stay here and make sure that the man doesn't go anywhere or hurts anyone else," he reasoned. "He could easily go through the other emergency door the opposite way."

The olive skinned woman quietly came forward to stand with the others. "You say he has hurt people?" she said with an accent Riley could not quite place.

"Not just hurt, he killed them!" the gothic teen said as black makeup continued to cascade down her face.

"Perhaps we should kill him? It'd be self-defense," the foreign woman reasoned, shrugging her shoulders. She wore a quartz necklace that made a soft tinkling sound as she moved.

"Whoa, whoa, whoa, I'm not killing anyone!" said the red haired man, jabbing his thumb into his mustard colored sweater. "For all I know you guys are the crazy ones!"

The black man took a step forward, glaring into his face. "All you need to do is look through that god damn window to know we aren't crazy," he snarled.

"Get out of my face!" the red haired man barked and pushed his palms against the man's chest.

Within seconds, the black man grabbed him by the collar of his sweater and shoved him. Surprised, the red haired man stumbled backwards, tripping on his own feet. His body fell into the emergency door, his head making contact with the window with a sharp crack.

Nancy flung herself between the two of them with her arms stretched out and her palms up. "Hey!" she snapped angrily. "Attacking each other is going to get us nowhere!"

The red haired man rubbed at the back of his head, a scowl on his face. The black man took a deep breath then looked down at Nancy with a curt nod.

"Okay," he said, breathing out. "Okay."

Riley ran a hand through her cropped brown hair, trying desperately not to think about getting high. Such a situation would tempt any addict, she was sure.

"Maybe we should move to the next car?" she suggested. "I doubt all of the intercoms are broken, and if we can contact the conductor, he can reach out to the police."

The Asian man nodded his head vigorously in agreement, but the black man frowned down at the ground.

"I think if we were to keep moving, panic would spread. You saw what happened to that woman when she was paralyzed with fear," he reasoned, crossing his arms across his muscular chest. "I think as long as we know where the man is, we should remain here."

"I don't want to die...," murmured the teen girl, her black hair falling around her face as she stared mournfully into her lap.

"Nobody else is fucking dying, alright?" Riley growled. "That man, whatever happened to him, looks messed up in the head."

"Well, obviously—"the black man interjected.

"No, I meant that he doesn't seem to be high functioning anymore," Riley said, cutting him off. "I don't know what happened, but I think the cognitive parts of his brain aren't working."

Nancy blinked at Riley, surprised to hear her very own thoughts come out of her daughter's mouth.

"I agree," Nancy murmured—which made Riley look surprised in turn.

"Well, that's great and all, but what are we going to do?" snapped the freckled man.

Suddenly, the emergency door on the opposite side of the train was opened and a blonde man, who appeared to be in his forties, poked his head into the car.

"Everything alright?" he asked. "We've been hearing a lot of yelling," he pointed behind him with his thumb.

The Asian man shook his head while the teen visibly shivered.

"No, man," said the black man with a grimace. "A man has started attacking and eating people. We have him isolated in the next car. Seems to be some kind of virus or infection."

The blonde man blinked at him. Riley could see his Adam's apple bob nervously above his teal colored necktie. "He's.... eating people?" he repeated, just barely above a whisper.

"Yes," Nancy nodded. "And we've been trying to contact—"

But the blonde man had shut the door with a definitive slam. Riley and Nancy watched, their jaws flying open, as the man locked the door behind him. He continued to look through the window, his expression a mixture of sorrow and resolve.

"Hey!" the black man growled, reaching the door in a couple of strides. He pounded his fist against the wall, staring at the blonde man as if he could kill him with his eyes.

"Open the door!" he demanded.

The blonde man stared back, his mouth turned down at the corners. He slowly shook his head. "I'm sorry," he mouthed. "Not safe."

The teen stared at the man from his seat, her blue eyes wide with fear. "Oh my god, we're gonna die!" she wailed and began to cry with renewed fury.

Hesitantly, the Asian man slowly moved his arm around the girl's shoulder, patting her awkwardly. To his surprise, she turned into his embrace, resting her head into the crook of his neck.

"Hopefully they contact the conductor in that car," Riley said, still staring at the blonde man. He had the decency to look sheepish as they made eye contact.

The black man slammed his fist against the door again, then turned his back to it. He sat down in the nearest seat and rested his elbows on his legs. He shook his head over and over again.

Nancy sighed, trying to suppress the rising panic she felt deep in her gut. "Okay," she said to herself. "Okay, let's think…"

She began to pace in a small circle on the brown floor of the train. Everyone was quiet apart from the teen, who continued to sob into the Asian man's shoulder.

The red haired man, who had been leaning against the wall with his arms crossed, suddenly lifted an index finger. "What if we pull the emergency brake? The conductor will instantly be notified that something is wrong," he said.

Riley shook her head, scratching at her skin. "The emergency brake should only be pulled when we are beside a platform," she argued. "If we pull the brake now, we will be stuck in this tunnel and police won't be able to reach us."

Nancy frowned up at the ceiling. Above the sound of the teenager's sobs, she heard a faint tinkling sound, like the first sprinkling of rain on a window. The train was still underground, enveloped in a tunnel of concrete.

The teen opened her mouth to speak, but Nancy shushed her, holding her hand up in the air. "Hold on," she said. "Do you guys hear that noise? What is that?"

Everyone sat still, their eyes unfocused as they concentrated on the sound.

"Where is that coming from?" Riley asked, looking out the window behind her.

Within seconds the noise became louder. Nancy and the other passengers watched in horror as pieces of glass fell from the cracked window of the emergency window. The sick man had somehow realized that the window had been broken, and was trying to crawl through.

"Ahh!" the Asian man cried and stood up from his seat. He grabbed onto the teen's black lacy shirt and pulled her with him towards the other end of the car as she screamed.

Within seconds, the black man was back on his feet, frantically rapping his knuckles against the emergency door the blonde man had gone through. "Open up!" he cried. "The man is coming in, open up!"

The passengers of the train looked at him and then to the blonde man. He sat in the first seat beside the emergency door, adjusting the collar of his shirt nervously. He was shaking his head, speaking to his fellow passengers. None of them looked happy, but they each nodded their heads, keeping their gaze down at the ceiling.

They weren't willing to risk their own lives to save anyone else.

"What do we do? What do we do?" asked the olive skinned woman, clutching at the seat in front of her with white knuckles.

"I...I'll try to take care of it," said the red haired man. He fished into the pocket of his jeans and pulled out a Swiss army knife.

The sick man had already burrowed through the window, seemingly not concerned that shards of glass were digging into his skin as he crawled through and fell to the floor head first. He growled and stood up again, looking at the passengers of the train with a hungry look in his eyes.

The red haired man clutched at his small knife and took a deep breath. With a noise of resolve, he ran forward, raising the knife up high above his head in a striking motion.

The freckled man sunk the knife deep into the man's neck as he bent forward, sinking his teeth into his forearm. Blood began to spurt from the knife wound, but the sick man still didn't seem to notice. He used the weight of his body to pull the red haired man down the ground. Hearing the man's screams made bile rise in Riley's throat.

Nancy took the steps to go from one side of the train to the other, hovering beside the black man. "You're the strongest one here, do you think you can break one of the side windows with your feet? We could get onto the roof!"

The man nodded and turned, raising his right black boot towards his waist. He gritted his teeth together as he kicked out against the glass over and over again.

"Oh god," the teenaged girl said, watching the red haired man scream and struggle against the sick man's mouth. She bent over and vomited on the floor at her feet.

Riley stared at the knife, which still protruded from the sick man's neck as he continued to attack the freckled man. "Everyone, pull out anything and everything in your pockets and bags that could be used as a weapon" she ordered.

Nancy looked down at her purse, surprised to see that it was still securely on her shoulders. She dug into the soft brown leather, feeling around until her fingers felt the long metal nail file she always kept in there.

The goth teen took off her spiked collar and wrapped it around her fingers so the spikes faced outward.

Riley had never liked purses, and typically carried her ID and phone in her jeans. She felt the outsides of her pockets, but the only thing she had on her person was a blue Bic lighter.

The overhead lights shut off as the passengers continued to search through their belongings. There were small yellow colored lights every few feet in the tunnel, but the car was mostly dark.

Nancy peered through the darkness, watching as the sick man continue to ingest the freckled man. His victim had stopped moving and making noise...

She let out a noise of despair and turned her attention back to the black man, who grunted as he thrust his boot against the window over and over again.

"Hurry!" she begged him, frantically waving her arms.

"I am!" he growled and thrust his foot against the window. The glass finally gave way. It broke into several pieces, some of which fell into the train while others fell out onto the tunnel. Riley could hear some of the shards crunch underneath the tracks of the train cars.

"Okay," she told herself and ran to where her mother stood. With deft fingers she snatched the nail file out of her mother's hand and held it as though it were a knife.

"Help everyone through the window," Riley yelled to her. "I'll take the rear."

Nancy shook her head, staring at her daughter by the faint yellow glow. "Absolutely not," she said.

"There's no time to argue, just do it!" Riley screamed back. She waved at everyone toward the very back of the car.

The black man was already halfway through the window, slowly raising his body up, careful not to scrape himself against the rough cement walls of the subway.

The Asian man helped keep the teen steady as they stood in front of the broken window. The woman with the olive toned skin had her hands out by the frame, prepared to help the black man in case he lost his balance. Nancy watched as his torso disappeared, then his thighs. All that was left on the frame were his worn black boots.

"Once I get up there, I will reach down and help everyone up!" he bellowed to the passengers below him.

He laid his body flat against the metal frame of the L train. The roof had thin grooves etched into the metal, but they weren't deep enough for the man to hold onto. He stared down the tunnel, trying to grip the train as it began to go around a sharp bend. Despite his strength, he could not find a good handhold on the metal.

"Shiiiiiiiit!" he cried, as his body began to slip sideways. He dug his fingernails into the metal but they were sweaty and betrayed him.

Nancy, Riley, and the other passengers stared in terror as the watched the black man's boots reappear, dangling from the roof of the train. They all tried to reach out for him, but the train swiftly turned, and his body moved with the momentum.

With one last agonizing cry, the black man lost his grip entirely and flew through the air. Gravity pulled him down until he tumbled onto the tracks...and was pulverized underneath the car that immediately followed.

"NOOO!" the teenaged girl shrieked, shaking her fists into the air as fresh tears careened down her pale cheeks.

"Oh my god," Nancy murmured as she poked her head out of the broken window. Blood was smeared along the bottom of the next car. Her stomach lurched and she forced herself to look away.

Inside the train, the sick man seemed to be tiring of his meal. Riley stared at his face, studying the way his eyes continued to yellow, and his skin seemed to go grey. "Guys, I think he's turning into a zombie," she murmured.

The Asian man gawked at her from beside the window. "Impossible," he said. "Zombies do not exist."

Riley watched as the sick man licked at the puddle of blood that had grown underneath the freckled man's body. "I think they do now," she said.

The woman with the olive toned skin walked to the nearest seat and set her black purse down. She rifled through it until she said "Aha!" and pulled out a crumpled piece of paper and a pen. In capital letters she wrote INFECTED MAN, PEOPLE DYING, PLEASE LET US IN. Once she was done, she tossed the pen over her shoulder and marched to the emergency door.

"Hey!" she yelled, and slammed the piece of paper against the window.

Nancy could make out a few people on the train from where she stood. The blonde man continued to sit in the chair closest to the door. He read the sign and swallowed again. Someone must have said something behind him because he turned in his chair and moved his arms about as though he were arguing.

The passengers watched as the pedestrians of the other car gestured wildly, and debated. Riley felt dread creep up her body from the tips of her toes as she tried to read their lips. If it had been her, she would have been at that door in the span of two seconds, cranking it open, saving lives.

It seemed that some people on the train felt the very same. They pointed at the sign, visible tears in their eyes as they yelled at the man in the suit.

After a few minutes of this, the blonde man moved his arms up and down as if to calm everyone. He spoke for a few minutes and then people began to raise their hands.

They were voting.

Nancy tried to count the hands, but it hardly mattered. She couldn't tell which hands voted for what. What was sickening was how close both rounds seemed to be...

The blonde man finished counting and nodded his head. He reached into the pocket of his dark grey suit and pulled out his cell phone. He worked his fingers on the screen then brought the phone over to the window. He had it open to a text message which read,

SORRY U GUYS COULD BE CONTAGIOUS TOO. MORE DEATH.

The teen lurched forward and vomited again, splattering her shiny black Doc Martens.

Fed up, Riley walked to the door. She stared at the blonde man, wishing—not for the first time in her life—that she could set fire by sheer will alone. His mouth was grim, but his eyes were guarded, almost steely as he looked back.

He did not want this to happen to them. But he was not willing to risk his own life to save anyone else's, either.

Riley slowly raised both hands and stuck her middle fingers up. If she was going to die, she was going to die without whimpering.

She was going to die fighting.

Suddenly, her mother was beside her, pulling her arms back down. Riley was about to snarl at her, but she looked up at Nancy's face and knew her mother wasn't trying to chastise her. Nancy's eyes were wide but steady as she looked down at her daughter.

"I just wanted to tell you that I love you," she murmured, gently putting a hand underneath Riley's chin.

"I... I never meant for anything like this to happen," Riley whispered back, feeling tears begin to well at the bottom of her eyes.

Nancy looked into her daughter's green eyes, and knew what she meant. She meant that she never meant to get addicted to heroin. She never meant to cause problems for her family.

She had never meant to cause any of them pain.

"I know," Nancy said, forcing her mouth into a weak smile. "I know."

A strange gurgling sound caused everyone to look at the opposite end of the train. The zombie was staring up at them from the meager remains of the red haired man—some fragments of his sweater and a pile of bloody, half eaten organs.

The zombie gurgled again. Blood oozed from the corners of his mouth, down onto his chin. His eyes were neon yellow in color, and no longer contained any semblance of human emotion in their irises.

With mechanical movements, the zombie steadily rose to his feet. His eyes trailed from one passenger to another, looking at each as though they were a dish laid out on the dinner table. He stepped through the remains of the corpse, intent on selecting his next victim.

The passengers huddled together at the other end of the train. The woman with olive skin began to pound her fists against the window, tears streaming down her cheeks as she begged them to open the door.

The teen girl whispered a prayer under her breath, her eyes closed. The Asian man stood beside her, muttering under his breath in Vietnamese.

It seemed that everyone was giving up.

Riley gritted her teeth and walked to the broken window. Carefully she grabbed the largest shard of glass she could find. It looked almost like a thunderbolt, narrowing to a sharp point at one end. She could feel its edges bite into her palm, but she just took a deep breath and gripped it all the more tightly.

She turned to look at her mother.

"I don't think we can take him on alone, but we if work together...."

Nancy sucked in a deep breath, and looked from the zombie down to the shard of glass clutched in her daughter's hand.

"No matter what, I am not getting off this train without you," Riley insisted vehemently. "Either we work together and try to kill him, or we die trying. We die together."

Nancy looked at the resolve in her daughter's eyes and felt a tear spill down her right cheek. She didn't want to die, but as she faced her potential—likely inevitable end—she was surprised to find she was not afraid. Her tears were for her daughter, for her courage, for her selflessness. She saw a layer of depth and beauty she had never noticed before, etched into the planes of her daughter's face.

At last Nancy nodded, brushing at her tears with an impatient hand. "Together," she said.

And she, too, grabbed a large shard of glass.

They resolved to flank the zombie, hoping having two people approach him would cause him to remain unsure and unfocused. Riley felt as though her heart would leap up her chest and out of her throat at any moment, it pounded so furiously.

As she stepped forward, a fraction of her brain imagined how things would have pained out if she had had heroin coursing through her veins at the time of the first attack. She would have been dead. She would have been killed and eaten and her mother would have had to have watched it all.

I'm never getting high again, she told herself.

"Where should we strike first?" Nancy asked. She tried to keep her voice steady as she walked forward.

"Let's gouge his eyes out first," Riley said. "We will have the advantage if he can't see."

She saw her mother nod in her periphery.

"On three?" Riley said, looking to her mother. She forced her mouth into a smile, one last attempt at bravado.

"On three," Nancy repeated.

"1... 2... 3!" Mother and daughter said in unison and raced forward, holding the glass high above their heads.

The zombie growled, clumsily bringing his arms forward. His sickly yellow eyes darted between both of them, seemingly unsure as to who to attack first. It was this hesitation that Riley had been banking on. She cried out as she lunged forward, and swung her arm forward. She used the momentum to gather power behind her strike and thrust the glass deep into the man's left pupil.

On the right, Nancy was doing the same thing. She wasn't as physically strong as her daughter, so she twirled in a tight circle, swinging her arm out wide to strike against the zombie. The glass sunk into his iris with a nauseating noise.

The zombie howled in pain, taking several steps backward as he frantically waved his arms about. He recognized that he was in pain, but seemed incapable of removing the glass from his eyes.

"Now, let's grab them back out and strike him!" Riley cried out. Blood ebbed from her hand as she grappled the glass, but she did not register the pain. Adrenaline coursed through every vein in her body.

Mother and daughter held onto their shards and repeatedly stabbed them into the sallow, grey flesh of the zombie's body. They struck at his heart and chest over and over again as he shrieked in agony. His stab wounds grew and spread as they worked, until it became one huge, gaping wound above his ribcage.

The zombie faltered, his bloody eyes turned toward the ceiling as he began to sway in place. Riley extended one of her black Chuck Taylor's and kicked the man until he fell to the ground. His limbs spread out half-hazardly across the brown floor, unmoving.

Nancy stared down at the zombie, her eyes wide, unable to process what had happened. Beside her, Riley fished into the back pocket of her jeans and pulled out the blue Bic lighter.

"For good measure," she said and cranked the metal wheel. She placed the flame against the man's clothing until it caught fire.

"Look! We are approaching a platform!" the teen girl said, pointing out the window to the left hand side. Sure enough, Nancy could see the platform careening ever closer.

"Hit the emergency brake!" she ordered, pointing at the red lever beside the main entry doors to the train.

The Asian man leapt forward and grabbed the lever, pulling it with both hands until it gave way.

As the train came to a screeching halt, Riley felt her mother's arms come around her in a hard embrace. Riley smiled, flinging her arms around her mother's shoulders in turn. They were together and they were alive.

END

DEAD EYES

Sunrise – the time of day when all the nightmarish atrocities of the world disappear like they were just figments of a teenage girl's imagination. The time of day where running from a horde of blood crazed lunatics seems far-fetched and completely bogus. The time of day where even the most feverish mind can take a step back and think, yes, the world is a beautiful and righteous place.

Mac wasn't prone to such bullshit, though. Oh no, she had learned early on in the game that stopping to smell the flowers and appreciate a pretty sunrise was the easiest way to get your legs caught in a stiff's teeth. *Never let 'em outta your sight,* her dad had always said. She intended to follow that bit of advice until the cows came home. In fact, she intended to follow every bit of advice Lt. Harry Wilson had ever given her.

The early morning air was nice and cool on her face as her feet hit the pavement. She'd camped out on a second story the night before. *Doors barred, instant street access if you need it, Mackey.* She wanted to write down all the survival gems her dad had given her over the last few months, maybe even give it a catchy title like *How to stiff a stiff* or *Lt. Harry Wilson's guide to avoiding death*. It was something she kept her mind busy with late at night when she heard scratching at the door, or when she waited behind a dumpster until she heard those god awful guttural noises they made pass into a different alleyway.

At present there were no stiffs prowling about in the street below, so she found it as good a time as any to be on her merry way. Her cherry red Doc Martens (a size too big, but who cared when the world was ending) were the perfect shoes for stealthy morning walks – they were quiet *and* properly attached to her feet. No tripping allowed in this part of town. And this part of town was *bleak*. The first reports on the news which mentioned the word *zombie* were some two months ago. Mac was surprised by the rate at which everything had gone to complete and utter shit after that. Her dad had said that society would survive this.

"Mackey," he said as he loaded up their SUV with water canisters, "civilization is too mighty a foe to conquer, you'll see."

Well, she did see. And what she was seeing as she walked the dusty debris-laden streets of Tallahassee wasn't a victorious civilization. It was a shit hole. Cars were parked in the street at all angles, some with their doors open. Others were still housing their owners now eternally clawing at the windows as she walked past.

"Want me to crack a window?" she asked as she walked past a particularly swollen looking woman snapping her teeth at the glass. The string of pearls around her neck looked about ready to snap, and Mac wasn't left disappointed. All the excitement of seeing breakfast walk past her Chevrolet prison caused the stiff to wriggle around like an eel in a bucket, providing that final bit of strain on the necklace, sending pearls bouncing off against the closed window and into the stiff's lap.

"Better get those fixed," Mac snorted and moved on.

She knew they were dead. She wasn't talking to them to reach their souls or whatever. She wasn't stupid. She was just tired of having no one to talk to. She hadn't been popular in school and preferred books to people, so it wasn't like she was a recovering socialite. But after spending her thirteenth birthday alone on the roof of K-Mart, she felt like it was time to start making conversation, even if they weren't talking back. She didn't know if Lt. Harry Wilson would agree. He was iffy on the subject of other people. One thing he had said as they drove through a small town somewhere east of San Francisco was, "People need other people. That's why we're going to Orlando. There are people there. Not stiffs, Mackey, but *real* people. They've made a stand. They have a type of barrier which keeps the dead out. Grammy and Bill are there."

She had no idea how her dad had known that her grandparents were in Orlando. At the time she filed it under *Stuff Lt. Harry Wilson knows through his divine knowledge of pretty much everything.* Mac felt something run down her cheek and wiped it away instinctively. Her fingers were wet when she looked at them. She had cried so much over the last two weeks that she wasn't even aware of it happening anymore. She sniffed and lifted her chin higher, daring her eyes to shed one more bloody tear.

She was hot and sweaty by the time she spotted a convenience store looking a little less menacing in the glare of the sun. The map her dad had left her put her on the eastern outskirts of Tallahassee. They'd come a long way from San Francisco, on a journey which would have only taken about three days to complete had they kept their SUV and not run into a million obstacles on the way. She was alone now, and the moving was slow. But if she kept to the road she could probably reach Orlando in a week or so.

Her backpack was alarmingly light as she set it down next to her on the floor of the convenience store called Stop 'n Go – exactly what she intended to do straight after she had a little browse. She went into Lt. Harry Wilson mode without giving it much thought.

Be quiet. They're not hiding from you – you're hiding from them. One thing you can count on is that the sons of bitches won't be stealthy. They make a lotta noise, and if you're quiet, you can hear them comin' before they get a whiff of you.

Mac sat down on her haunches and waited, the door directly behind her if she needed to make a quick exit. The smell in the store was a sickening combination of rotting meat and expired produce. She hadn't made a lot of noise coming in, but if anything had heard her, it would be making its way down one of the aisles towards the sound. They were attracted to sound like moths to a flame. She knew that all too well.

It was a small store with six aisles, and she could easily see the freezer lined back wall.

Don't get cocky. Just cos you can't hear them, doesn't mean they're not there. Secure the place one aisle at a time.

Slowly and quietly she walked to the wall on her left, taking care to avoid any of the broken glass scattered on the tiles.

Watch your feet.

She cast a quick glance behind the cashier's counter and stopped dead in her tracks. A shotgun was lying on the floor in a mess of putrefying body parts. The previous owner had died with the gun in his hand – virtually the only part of his body not clawed and chewed at. It hadn't been an easy death, that much was obvious.

Make a note of anything you can use, but don't get comfortable. Secure the building before raiding it.

The far left aisle was clear of both the dead and anything useful. She didn't need shampoo or toilet paper, it would only weigh down her backpack and give the stiffs something to smell. Her stomach agreed in a sudden fit of gurgles. She retraced her steps back to the front of the store.

There's no point in walkin' the store like you're killin' time, Mackey. Stay close to the exit. Your eyes know what they're lookin' for.

The second aisle's shelves were not so disappointing. Dried beans, sugar, and macaroni were strewn across the floor. She saw a few discarded cans lodged underneath the metal shelf, and made another mental note. The rest of the store was empty. No stiffs, and no buffet of hamburgers and ice cream. A girl could dream.

Mac quickly made her way to the cans she had seen, her Docs crunching over the sugar and macaroni on the floor. She studied her plunder: Old El Paso Jalapeno slices, Green Giant whole kernel sweet corn, Bush's Best Boston recipe baked beans, Campbell's Chunky New England clam chowder and a cracked bottle of Smuck's sweet orange marmalade leaking its contents onto her hand.

Take what you can, and get out. Don't burden yourself with anythin' you can't carry off easily. If you have to run, drop everything, and haul ass. Your life is worth more than a can o' beans.

She was busy stuffing the cans into her backpack when she heard a door creak. Her breath caught in her throat as she went completely still. A dragging sound came from the far right corner of the store, and with it, the ragged choking sound reserved for the living dead. Mac glanced towards the cashier's counter, painfully aware of the shotgun lying only a few feet away from her. If she was quick she could get it and be out of the door before the stiff even knew she was there. Should she risk it? A gun could mean the difference between life and death. 250 miles left to Orlando. Who knew what would be waiting on the road.

She jumped up and snuck over to the expired shop keep without making a sound. It took her a few seconds to wrench the gun from his stiff cold fingers. She was just about to poke her head from behind the counter when she heard the sound of sugar and macaroni crunching under heavy feet. Her body went numb. The stiff was *much* closer than she had anticipated. She heard the door creak again.

Shit! she mouthed.

There were at least two of them now, maybe more. Why didn't she secure the door when she spotted it earlier? Lt. Harry Wilson would shit his pants if he could see her now.

She clutched the gun to her chest. It was loaded, but she wouldn't risk firing it in here unless she had absolutely no other choice.

If you think breakin' some glass or bangin' a door shut draws them in, just imagine what gunfire does. Easiest way to get yourself killed. Reserve gunfire for the most critical of situations, Mackey. Don't you fire that thing unless you're sure that 1) you can get the hell out of there once you've pulled the trigger, and 2) whatever you're shootin' at isn't gonna get up again.

Mac wasn't sure of either of those.

Her brain was working rapidly. She'd have to see what was happening on the other side of the counter before she could fully assess the situation. She was going to have to risk a glance around the corner. But she didn't have to. Just as she was about to move into a kneeling position, something rounded the bend at the far end of the store, coming up the aisle directly next to the counter. There was nowhere she could hide.

The stiff shuffling along the aisle had been a teenager when he got bit. He was wearing a red apron with the words *Stop 'n Go* printed in cheerful white letters on the front. Half of his face was missing, and his teeth were clearly visible through the hole in his cheek. His eyes were two milky white globes in a mess of rotting black flesh. With each labored step chunks of skin swayed rhythmically from his jawbone on the side of his face which had evidently been eaten off by his killer. It seemed to Mac like an entire lifetime had passed by the time his dead seeing-but-unseeing eyes spotted her. He snapped out of his docile state and barreled down the aisle towards her, his teeth snapping against each other so hard she could hear them cracking.

She had no choice but to jump up and over the counter. She felt his fingers get caught in her hair just as her feet touched the ground. With a painful yank of her head she tore free from his grasp, probably leaving a bit of her scalp behind. The other stiff came at her from another aisle, but she was quicker than its outstretched arms. In one swift movement, she grabbed her backpack from the floor and pushed through the door, her hands around the gun in an iron grip.

She sprinted down the street. The commotion in the store was bound to attract others, she had to get out of the area, and fast.

She rounded a corner and nearly dropped the gun. There was a whole horde of them shuffling aimlessly down the street. Cars were parked on either side of the road, creating an undead funnel straight towards her. No wonder she hadn't seen any that morning – they were all congregating in one bloody spot. They noticed her almost immediately, and before she could so much as catch her breath, an entire crowd of them came running at her down the road. She backed up into the street she'd come from, only dimly aware of another stiff in a red apron coming at her from the direction of the Stop 'n Go.

She ran.

Put as much distance between you and them as possible. One stiff attracts another. If they can see you, they're gonna chase you.

Mac sifted through every bit of advice Lt. Harry Wilson had ever given her, but came up short. All she could do was run. Her brain was preoccupied with the sole purpose of getting the hell out of there.

She had put quite some distance between herself and the horde when powerful hands grabbed her from below. Excruciating pain shot through her arm as a pair of yellow decayed teeth sank into her wrist. The shotgun clattered onto the tarmac as she pressed the palm of her free hand onto the rotting face of her attacker. She could feel the skin and flesh move under her hand against the stiff's skull as she shoved his head back. The lower half of his body was gone. His torso had been lying in wait in front of the car as she ran past. Her arm came free of his teeth, but only after he had managed to take a giant chunk of it. She stepped back, looking down at her arm in horror. Blood gushed from the wound onto the ground. She was in shock. The dead thing was clawing its way across the road to her, his teeth clattering together. With revulsion she saw bits of her own flesh lodged between its teeth.

For the second time that day unseen hands grabbed her, this time from behind. But this stiff had somehow retained the ability to speak, cos it was saying something to her.

"Move!" it shouted.

She turned her head. What a peculiar stiff this was. His eyes weren't all milky and messed up either.

"We have to move!" it said again, grabbing her by the shoulder.

She snapped out of her daze and nodded. She followed him through a maze of side streets and alleyways until he burst through a fire door on the side of a large office space. Once inside he barred the door with a heavy desk and turned to look at her. He was young, probably the age of apron-boy, but his face was lined and grim like he'd seen the end of the world. Mac wondered what her face looked like.

"Sit down," he said, motioning to a leather swivel chair next to another desk. She sat. She seemed to have lost the ability to speak or to make her own decisions. Yup, she was definitely in shock. The pain in her arm was throbbing violently, blackening the edge of her vision.

"I'm sorry," he said as he stood in front of her, "but we have to do this quickly."

In one sudden movement, he raised a machete above his head. Mac only had a brief moment to see it glint in the ray of sunlight shining through the window before it landed on the desk next to her with a dull thud. She looked down at it, surprised at the widening pool of blood forming on the polished surface. It was only after she saw her own severed hand twitching on the other side of the blade that the darkness overtook her completely and she passed out.

...

"Mac, get out of here!" her dad shouted.

He was leaning against the door, holding the crowd of undead on the other side of it at bay.

"Dad, I'm not leaving you!" she screamed back.

"Mac, listen to me!" sweat was running down his forehead into his eyes as he strained against the door, the horrible sound of fingernails against wood chilling her to her very core, "you have to go. Take my bag. The map is there, everything is there. Go to Orlando."

"Dad, we can make it!"

"Mac!" the door opened slightly, but he managed to bang it shut again, "Please, baby, you have to go. I can't hold them for much longer. You can climb out the window, there's a fire escape."

Mac looked to where he dad was motioning with his head, but she couldn't do it. She couldn't leave him. If he was going to stay, then so was she. They would die together.

"Mac," he said as if reading her mind, "No. You have to go. You have to stay alive!"

"Daddy," she cried, "I can't do it without you."

"Yes you can, baby," tears were rolling down his cheeks, "You're so strong! Remember what I've told you, Mackey. Now go!"

"Dad!" giant sobs were wracking her body.

"I love you, Mackey."

"I love you too, daddy."

Mac jerked awake, a scream lodged in her throat.

"It's okay," someone said from next to her, "You're okay."

The room was dark except for a single burning candle. Mac was lying on a pile of blankets, her body drenched in sweat and shivering. She looked up into the face of the guy who had saved her. The guy who had cut off her hand.

"You must be hungry," he said, walking over to the candle. The smell of cooking food made her stomach rumble shamelessly and loudly.

"Does that answer your question?" she asked in a hoarse voice.

He smiled at her over his shoulder. She could feel the weight of her arms next to her body, but she refused to look down at the one the stiff had sunk his teeth into. She couldn't bear to see a stump right now. Not yet. She was mercifully free of any pain whatsoever.

"I hope you don't mind," he said as he lifted an empty can of Campbell's Chunky New England clam chowder, "I staked out that store for two days before you came down on it in one fell swoop."

He chuckled as he dished some of the chowder into a coffee mug missing a handle.

"Sorry about that," she croaked.

"Don't be," he replied kindly, "We all have to take care of ourselves the best we can now. What with the world going to shit and all."

He placed the mug on a wooden tray and carried it over to her. With some maneuvering, he helped her to prop herself up against the wall and put the tray on her lap. Instinctively she reached for the tray with her left hand but found that there were no fingers to move. The end of her arm, where her hand used to be, was covered in thick white bandages. She could only stare at it for a while.

"You'll get used to it," he said as he sat cross-legged next to her.

"Are you a doctor or something?" she asked as she spooned some chowder into her mouth.

"Med student," he replied with a shrug.

They finished their meal in silence. Mac couldn't bring herself to consider the implications of traveling across the state with half of the hands she had yesterday. Orlando seemed further away than it had when she was on the other side of the country.

"What's your name?" he asked as he cleared away their dishes.

"Mac," she said, smiling weakly.

"I'm Kyle," he said, sticking out his hand but retrieving it almost immediately, looking embarrassed.

"Why doesn't it hurt?" she asked, lifting up her stump.

"Ah, that would be the super strong painkillers," he replied, "Being a med student gives you the advantage of knowing the good stuff from the *really* good stuff."

She chuckled, hoping he had a lot more where that came from.

"Is Mac short for something?" Kyle asked, the candlelight flickering across his face.

"Makayla," she replied, "but no one ever really calls me that."

"Where you headed?" he asked, lying down on his own pile of blankets and folding his arms behind his head.

"Orlando," she said with a sigh, "My grandparents are there."

"I heard it's safe there," he said, glancing at her.

"Yeah, it is," she moved down onto her back again, feeling extremely sleepy, "My dad and I, we've been traveling from San Francisco."

Kyle made a whistling sound through his teeth.

"That's a long way to go," he said.

"We've... I've made it this far."

She looked up at the ceiling and the intricate shadows the flickering candlelight created there. Lt. Harry Wilson was silent, muted by the drugs.

"You should get some sleep," Kyle said, getting up and moving towards the candle, "You've lost a lot of blood, but you're okay, the infection didn't get a chance to spread. We would have known by now if it had."

"Kyle," she said before closing her eyes and drifting off into a blessedly dream-free sleep, "Thank you."

...

"How much further?" Mac asked for the hundredth time that day.

"About ninety miles," Kyle replied patiently from the driver's seat.

She liked him. There were times when he reminded her of Lt. Harry Wilson, and that made her smile. They were only ninety miles from Orlando, and Mac was getting restless. Their last few days of traveling had seen insane amounts of rainfall. She wondered if the rain had any effect on the stiffs whatsoever, or if it just softened them up some more like overripe tomatoes baking in the sun.

The world is gonna be a green place after this, Mackey, what with all the fertilizer walkin' around.

"Shit, Mac," Kyle said from next to her, easing on the break of the Lexus they had lifted from a liquor store's parking lot. Some drunk had left the keys in the ignition, or that was at least the story Mac told herself.

The road was blocked by a camper lying on its side. Stiffs were ambling along around it like religious zealots around some kind of holy relic.

"We have to go around," Mac said almost automatically.

Protect the vehicle at all costs, Mackey. If it looks like trouble, go 'round if you can. Don't stop. There are things even worse than stiffs, unfortunately. But check the terrain before you do anythin' or you'll get your ass stuck in a marsh or your tires blown to hell or somethin' equally unpleasant.

"Wait," she said as Kyle started moving onto the dirt next to the road, "something doesn't feel right. Go back."

"Mac..." he started, but she interrupted him.

"Just trust me! Go back," she scanned the surrounding trees but saw nothing out of the ordinary - if you count walking corpses as ordinary, of course.

"Something about the camper wasn't right," she said as they drove back the way they came to yet another back road leading out of there, "I wonder how it got that way."

"Who knows," Kyle said, exasperated, "Maybe a bee flew in the window and stung the driver on his fucking eyeball."

Mac laughed, but Kyle didn't. This was the umpteenth time they had to turn around and go back the way they came to try another road. Their options were declining radically.

"I just didn't trust it," Mac said softly.

"Lt. Harry Wilson?" Kyle asked.

"Lt. Harry Wilson," she sighed.

Their humble abode for the evening was an abandoned farmhouse which looked to Mac like something out of The Amityville Horror, a movie she watched without her dad's knowledge and against his wishes. It was something which still gave her nightmares, though she would never admit it.

The sky was a dark and violent gray, the smell of an approaching storm in the air. They didn't have any food left, so their stomachs provided the background noise during the brief interludes of thunder silence.

They were only about 50 miles from Orlando, but they couldn't risk driving through the storm. They'd come this far, and to end it all now in some muddy car accident would have been the most rotten cherry on a cake of flesh.

Mac was telling Kyle about the book of wisdom she wanted to compile when a deep voice spoke behind them.

"Hands," it said, after which there was the distinct sound of a shotgun being cocked.

This must be some cosmic joke, Mac thought as she lifted her stump into the air.

"What have we got here, Roy?" another voice said.

"Two young lovers enjoying the end of the world," Roy responded.

Heavy footsteps creaked on the wooden floorboards.

"We don't want any trouble," Kyle said, casting a quick glance at Mac.

There may come a time when people are a greater threat than the undead. Be still, Mackey. Do what they want, and don't provoke them. Stay alive. But you keep your eyes open. Wait for them to reveal the weakness they inevitably have. Bid your time, and run.

"We don't want no trouble neither," deep voice said, "but we *do* want the keys to the car."

"Please," Mac found her voice, "we're going to Orlando. It's safe there. You can come with us."

Deep voice laughed.

"Hear that, Jamie? It's safe in Orlando."

Jamie made a noise which Mac could only associate with a pig rolling in shit. She cringed on the inside. The laughter died down and was followed by an intensely uncomfortable silence. Mac wished she could turn around and stare her assailants in the face. She hated feeling like a coward. Lt. Harry Wilson wouldn't have been a coward.

"Keys," deep voice said, "or we'll take them off your corpses."

"They're in my pocket," Kyle said nervously.

"Jamie, get."

More footsteps.

"Nice and easy now young pup," Jamie said as he fished the keys out of Kyle's pocket.

"Here's what's gonna happen," deep voice said authoritatively, "we're gonna go out the front door and close it nice and tight, do you folks a favor by not lettin' in the dead ones millin' about on the porch, and we're gonna drive on outta here without any trouble. Got it?"

Mac and Kyle nodded in unison.

"Roy," Jamie moaned, "the girl."

"Jamie, she's not..."

"You promised!"

"Okay, okay!"

The floorboards creaked again. Mac could feel the heat coming off the man standing behind her. She felt cold steel against her skin as he pressed the barrel of the gun against her neck.

"You're comin' with us," deep voice said.

"No, please," Kyle said, getting ready to stand up.

"Sit down!" Roy roared, chilling Mac's blood. She could tell he wouldn't think twice of shooting Kyle right in his face.

"You," he said, pushing the gun deeper into her neck, "Up. Now. Or we feed your boyfriend to our friends outside."

Mac got onto shaky legs, tears threatening in her eyes.

Don't be afraid, Mackey.

She turned around and faced one of the biggest men she had ever seen. His long black hair was tied back in a greasy ponytail. She gauged that four of her could fit inside one of him. Jamie was standing in the doorway, the opposite of Roy in appearance, but she thought she could bet her life on them being equally rotten on the inside.

"Let's go," he motioned to the door with his gun.

"Mac!" Kyle shouted as she reached the door, "I'm... sorry."

"It's not your fault," she managed before being huddled out of the house.

Roy and Jamie's *friends* came at them as soon as they stepped onto the porch, but their sluggish dead limbs were no match for her captors' guns. Their faces were smashed in as soon as they were within reaching distance. Mac looked back at the house as she was ushered into the back seat of the Lexus. Roy and Jamie had lied. They'd left the front door wide open. Mac screamed in horror as she saw two stiffs wander through the entrance, hoping Kyle could hear her.

Tears were streaming down her face as the farmhouse disappeared behind the trees.

"Quiet down, now," Roy said from the driver's seat.

"What do you want?!" Mac screamed at them.

Roy stepped on the break, causing Mac's face to smash into the seat in front of her.

"I said, quiet down!" Roy snapped, "Keep your mouth shut or I swear to Christ I will break your teeth."

Mac's lip trembled, but she held her tongue. Lt. Harry Wilson would do as they say until he could escape. Mac had never missed her dad more.

The sun was hanging low on the horizon, casting its orange light onto the dark clouds above them in beautiful shades of pink and purple. Mac hadn't stopped to appreciate the beauty of the world for quite some time, so she allowed her eyes to drink in all the magnificent colors of the sky. She had the nagging feeling that she wouldn't have the opportunity to do it again for a good long while.

"What's this?" Jamie asked, waking Mac from her thoughts.

They'd reach the same camper she and Kyle had come across earlier that day.

"We go 'round," Roy said simply.

He moved the Lexus onto the dirt next to the road, overtaking the camper at a dangerous speed. There was a deafening pop as the car swerved and slid over the dry mud. Roy cursed as he tried to straighten out the steering wheel, but the wheels had locked. Everything was moving in slow motion then. Mac saw the world outside of the car spin around and around until everything tipped and tumbled. Her head smashed first into the ceiling, and then into the window, then into the ceiling again.

It was a while before she realized that the car had come to a stop. The silence was deafening. Mac lay on the ceiling of the car, trying not to move anything.

Assess your injuries before trying to get out, Mackey.

Her ears were ringing and her head hurt something fierce, but Mac managed to move both her legs and arms. She turned her head to where Roy and Jamie had been, but they must have been flung through the windscreen because she was alone in the wreck.

Blessedly, her ears stopped ringing, and she could hear the wheels of the car still spinning aimlessly above her. There was also a sharp hissing sound she didn't recognize, probably some part of the engine destroyed in the roll. She heard another sound which made her stomach sink - the gurgled, throaty gagging of the dead. The missing windscreen was the easiest way out. Mac crawled over the broken glass, struggling with only one hand. Sharp shards cut at her knees and palm, but she pushed through. Her head was swimming by the time she finally escaped the car. Darkness threatened her vision, but she took a deep breath, refusing to pass out.

Bits of debris were lying on the ground around her. Her eyes searched the wreckage for Roy and Jamie, and when they finally found them she couldn't help but feel pity for the sons of bitches. They were lying a few feet from each other, arms outstretched like they had been reaching for one another in their final moments. Bent over them were half a dozen ghastly forms, each one in different states of decay. Her captors' intestines were spilled onto the dirt as the dead feasted on them.

Mac saw her opportunity and slipped behind the camper out of sight. She had two options – she could run in the direction of Orlando (so close she could almost taste it), or she could follow the road back to the farmhouse, back to Kyle. It was an easy decision.

The fact that she had escaped the crash with but a bump on the head was nothing short of a miracle, and the weight of the situation wasn't lost on Mac as she jogged down the road. The sun had almost set completely, and with it came the chill of the night. Thunder roared in the sky above, and a small drizzle began to fall. Mac pushed forward, her lungs burning. Every now and then she had to catch her breath and stop the dizziness from overtaking her. All she could think of was Kyle, and finding him alive and okay at the farmhouse.

Family, Mackey, is more important than anything. In this world, now, you have to find your own family. A family of strangers. But keep 'em close, like I keep you close.

Kyle was her family now. He was the only thing she had in the world now, and she would do anything to get back to him.

It felt like hours later when she finally spotted the farmhouse in the dim light reflected from the storm clouds above. It was raining, but not heavily. The wind had picked up, whipping the tree branches violently from side to side. Mac ran up the stairs to the front door, which was closed. She managed a relieved smile as she caught her breath and reached for the knob.

"Kyle!" she shouted as she entered the house, "Oh my god, I thought you were dead. I saw.."

The words caught in her throat. Kyle was standing in the doorway leading to the living room where earlier that day they had sat and laughed together. His face was sunken and pale, his skin drenched in an unhealthy sweat. A gaping wound on his shoulder was leaking blood onto his shirt and down his arm.

"Mac," he said, smiling weakly, "I didn't think I would ever see you again."

The words seem to take the last bit of his strength. His legs collapsed under him and he fell hard onto the floorboards. Mac ran to him. The wound on his shoulder smelled foul, like he was already starting to rot even though his heart was still beating.

"I got 'em, Mac," he said wheezily, "I killed the stiffs."

Mac laughed through the tears. Just a few days ago he had told her how barbaric a term that was.

"You're gonna be okay," she said with a sob, "You're okay."

But Kyle hadn't heard her. His eyes were staring past her, and his breathing had stopped. He was dead.

Mac put her head on his chest and screamed. Her only family taken away. Again. She was alone. Again. The world was a horrible stinking place, and she hated it.

She left the farmhouse in a daze, just as the storm hit properly. She wandered down the road aimlessly, unaware of the rain slamming against her body. She didn't fight when a figure came at her from amidst the trees. She didn't scream as rotting teeth sank into her skin.

...

A horde of the living dead wandered down the road to the heavily guarded roadblock just outside of Orlando. Soldiers sat in the sun on the wall, sweating in their weighty gear. The horde gurgled and groaned, but had nowhere to go. Among them was a young girl with one hand, cherry red Doc Martens shuffling in the dust.

CEMETERY THINGS by Jennifer Benn

Katie was sitting on the floor of her dorm room. Papers and books were strewn around her in an arc. So far, her junior year of college had consisted of nothing but all-nighters, energy drinks, and stress eating. Her roommate's television was blaring something about a revolutionary treatment for brain tumors. "Mia, could you turn that down please?" The racket made it hard to focus. She had already read the same sentence three times.

"Mia!" Katie yelled in frustration over the news anchors as she slammed down her chemistry book. The book's hardcover sounded like a gunshot as it struck the floor. Katie tugged her black t-shirt down as she stood up. She hooked her fingers into her belt loops and jumped a little as she wiggled her jeans higher on her hips. She stomped across the living room to Mia's bedroom. Her eyes bulged in annoyance as she glared from the doorway.

Mia had her toothbrush hanging out of her mouth. A slight, minty froth gathered at the corners of her lips. Damp hair clung to her shoulders from the shower, and the steam still lingered in the air. Mia was sitting on the edge of her bed. Her blue comforter and wet towel were in a heap on the floor. Mia's eyes were wide as she kept watching the screen. Light from the television played across her face as the scenes shifted. Katie walked over to her with an exasperated sigh and plopped down next her. The TV was looping footage of a brain cancer patient who had been undergoing the newest treatment. They called it Recusant. It was an injection that targeted the mutated tumor cells and shrank the cancer. Katie watched as the video clip showed a man whose skin was sallow and cheeks were sunken in. Her frustration melted into horror as she watched, both repulsed and fascinated at the same time. She couldn't make herself look away. The patient looked more skeleton than a man. His eyes were wide and crazed as they darted back and forth hardly blinking. The tendons in his neck threatened to snap and burst free as he strained against his hospital bed. The orderlies were trying to secure his restraints, but the man lashed out at them. A nurse ran in to help hold him down, and the man sunk his teeth into her forearm. The footage cut off abruptly and looped back to the beginning. The pane zoomed out to show the reporter in the studio while the hospital footage continued in the top, right-hand corner.

"Nurse Lee is still in critical condition and has begun to show signs of brain damage in her prefrontal cortex. Doctors caring for the injured nurse say that this area of the brain is responsible for behavior and personality. At this time, her cortex is being monitored by regularly scheduled MRI's, but specialists say there is a steady decrease in its size. Nurse Lee and the other patients who have undergone Recusant treatments are being closely monitored." The news anchor's voice remained emotionless through the story as she transitioned nonchalantly to the weather segment.

Mia turned slowly towards Katie. Her eyes welled up, and she pulled the dangling toothbrush out of her mouth with a shaking hand. Mia's mom had been one of the first patients in the trial study for the 'revolutionary scientific breakthrough of the century.' At first, it had been going well. There were improvements. There was even hope for a full recovery, but as the doses increased, the side effects became more apparent. Now, Mia had just seen a sneak peek at what was going to happen to her mother. Katie's heart sagged as she hugged Mia tightly through her sobs.

Katie's phone started ringing in her pocket. She pulled it out and saw Kacey's face on the screen. She hadn't kept in touch very well with her little sister since school had started back up. Guilt settled in the pit of her stomach. Kacey was in high school now. She played the flute in the marching band and was on the debate team. She had texted Katie a few times this semester and asked if she could make it to her recital or come watch her debate, but Kacey had been so overwhelmed with her classes that she had never even texted back. The guilt twisted in Katie's gut as she slid her finger over to ignore the call from her little sister.

She focused on rocking Mia gently. The rhythmic swaying helped to calm them both. Katie could feel warm tears seep into the shoulder of her t-shirt. Her roommate's muffled cries were punctuated with sharp inhales as Mia's body tried desperately to remind her to breathe. Katie's phone rang again. "I've gotta take this." Katie's voice was gentle and comforting, but the guilt squirmed in her stomach, "I'll be right back, ok?" She gave her roommate an extra tight squeeze and handed her the teddy bear that was laying on Mia's pillow. Mia curled up on her bed and squeezed the bear to her chest, still rocking slightly. She reached out and took the picture frame from her bedside table and ran her finger over her mom's face. The glass had a light sheen of moisture from remaining humidity in the room. Her fingertip caused the glass to squeak as it skidded along the surface. The picture was from Mia's high school graduation. She and her mother had the same dark hair and the same slender build. People had always teased them that they could be sisters, but that was before the cancer had taken hold.

"Hello," Katie half whispered into her phone, "Kace, this isn't really a good—what? Wait. Slow down. Who's doing what now?"

Kacey's voice was panicked, "Some of the patients escaped! CDC has put up roadblocks and the town is under quarantine. They're attacking people! The news said they've already had two confirmed murders, and at least five are injured. Mom's out of town on business, and dad isn't answering his phone. I'm scared, Katie. I dunno what to do." Katie could hear her sister begin to hyperventilate.

"Whoa, hold on." Katie was trying to process all of this at once. People like that guy on TV were out roaming the streets, killing people, and Kacey was home alone. "Ok," she said trying to kick herself into adult mode, "lock the door. I'll be there as soon as I can. Don't let anyone in. Promise me."

"I...I promise." Kacey's voice faltered between her quick, shallow breaths.

"I mean it, Kace. No one." Katie hung up the phone. Her thoughts were racing. She had been a crappy sister the past few months, but this was more important than her studies. When it really counted, she had to be there for Kacey. The guilt in her stomach writhed and solidified into a formidable foundation of determination. Katie let out a slow, deep breath as she allowed the situation to sink in.

"Hey, Mia," Katie walked gently back to Mia's doorway trying to remain calm for her friend's sake, "I gotta go. Kacey needs me right now...are you going to be ok? Do you want me to call someone for you? Jack, maybe?" Mia's boyfriend wasn't the best at emotional support, but at least it was something. Katie's heart thudded and drummed against her ribs, but her external, placid façade remained in place.

Mia sat up still clutching her ragged, tear-stained bear, "Would it be ok if I just came with you?" Her voice was meek, and she looked so vulnerable.

Katie looked at her and weighed the options. This could be dangerous, and Mia wasn't in the right frame of mind to deal with that right now. She wasn't in the right frame of mind to be left alone either, though. If Katie left Mia behind, she would be worried about her and wouldn't be able to focus fully on taking care of Kacey. There was a rumble outside and the sound of screeching brakes. "What the hell?" Kacey strode over to the window. Military jeeps had started to form a perimeter around the campus. "Shit. Mia, grab your crap. We have to go."

"What is it?" Mia walked up to the window and saw the insignia on one of the vehicles. "Why is the National Guard here?"

Katie grabbed her backpack and dumped its contents on the floor. "Some of the Recusant patients escaped the hospital," she said while shoving an extra hoodie and a couple bottles of water into her bag. "Kace said they were putting up quarantines. Mom is out on business, and she can't get ahold of dad." Katie paused, "Do we have any weapons?" It was such a weird question to hear herself asking.

"Weapons?" Mia looked at Katie quizzically. "We have steak knives, but that's about it. Did...did she say which patients?" Mia had followed Katie into the kitchen. "Why do you need a weapon?" Mia's second question was an afterthought. Her mind was focused almost entirely on one uncertainty: Was her mother one of the escapees?

Katie stopped rifling through the silverware drawer and looked up at her friend. Mia was pale as she clutched the edge of the counter. "No," Katie's voice was empathetic, "she didn't say any names, but some of them have already hurt people. I just want to be prepared. Get together some clothes and anything else you want, ok? We have to leave before they get us all blocked in. We can call the hospital when we get to my parents' house and check on your mom."

Mia nodded meekly and went to her room to pack her things. Her arms stayed still at her side as she walked, trancelike, into her bedroom. Katie went back to looking through the kitchen drawers. Spoon, spoon, fork. "Where the heck are all of our frigging knives?" She mumbled to herself. She opened the dishwasher which was packed full of dirty dishes. The smell of caked on food busted free from the opening. "You've got to be kidding me." Katie wrinkled her nose, pulled out two of the cleanest looking knives in the silverware section, and started scrubbing them in the sink.

"Remain calm. Everyone stay in your dorms." A voice echoed from a speaker outside.

"Let's go, Mia!" Katie yelled from the kitchen while she wiped the knives off on a dish rag. She slung her backpack over her shoulders and grabbed a ball cap to cover her short, messy hair. Mia came out of her room with a duffle bag strap swung across her body. Her wet hair was tied up in a ponytail. Her green shirt was darker where her hair had dripped on it, and the hems of her blue jeans were frayed. Katie handed her a knife.

"You really think we're going to need these?" Mia held the knife pinched between her middle finger and thumb like it was a dirty diaper she couldn't wait to throw away.

"I would rather have it and not need it than need it and not have it," Katie said matter-of-factly as she opened the dorm door and poked her head out into the hallway. Students were wandering to both exits trying to see what was going on outside. Katie held open the door and let Mia step into the hall before following. She turned and looked around their room before closing and locking the door behind them. The click of the lock had a ring of finality to it. Katie grabbed Mia's shoulders, turning her so that they were looking one another in the eye. "Stay close."

Mia nodded and tried to conceal her panic. The two of them shouldered past their classmates until they reached the glass door that led to the campus grounds. A crowd had already gathered. "I guess no one told the National Guard the best way to get college kids to go somewhere is to either tell them not to go there or offer them free food," Katie said under her breath while she kept an eye on the commotion. There was a soldier placed every two feet across the main entrance to the campus. They kept shifting nervously. Their posture was casual, and even from this far away Katie could tell their boots weren't up to spec. She grew up as a military brat. Her dad was a Marine, and they had lived on military bases most of her life. These weren't combat-tested soldiers, hardened and ready to kill if necessary. These poor guys had barely made it out of basic. They looked like they should be at a frat party, not lined up like a firing squad. Katie tightened her grip on her knife and kept it close to her side as she and Mia walked in the opposite direction from the crowd.

"Miss? Excuse me, miss?" One of the soldiers had spotted them.

"Keep going. Don't look back." Katie grabbed Mia's arm and pulled her along faster. They were almost off the grass. The sidewalk was only a few feet away.

"Miss!" He was approaching them with his gun firmly grasped in both hands. The barrel gleamed in the afternoon sun as he held it upright. Katie could see him out of the corner of her eye. He had dark hair, and his broad shoulders were slumped forward slightly. His long legs were closing the gap. Katie quickened her pace.

Suddenly, an ear-splitting scream cut through the air. The crowd of students started scattering, and gunshots rang out. Katie and Mia instinctively turned towards the sounds and saw three people in St. Mary's hospital gowns near the soldiers. It looked like one of the of the soldiers had tried to talk the patients into backing down, but they had lunged forward and bit him. The guardsmen were now firing at the patients. The bullets didn't seem to faze them. The patients kept chewing on him, and chunks of his flesh made sickening, wet, smacks on the sidewalk as they tore him apart. The soldier who had called out to them earlier looked torn between returning to his ranks or securing the girls. He squared his jaw and locked eyes with Katie.

He sprinted determinedly towards her just as one of the patients grabbed a freshman girl and sank her teeth into the tender flesh of the girl's shoulder. "Let's move!" he yelled at them. His booming voice jolted Katie out of her disbelief at what was happening, and she followed him as he ran past. Mia was still shocked by the massacre that was unfolding in front of the school.

"Mia!" Katie yelled over her shoulder. Mia snapped out of her trance and forced her legs to move.

The three of them ran down Main Street until they were three blocks away from the college. The further into town they got, the more disaster they saw. Bodies were strewn between the stores. Some people were still alive. Thick, sticky blood spurted with every heartbeat from a man who was clutching a gash in his thigh. A pool of blood was forming quickly around him. Those who hadn't been mauled by the Recusant patients were either trying to stem the bleeding of the living or taking this opportunity to loot for personal gain. The chaos brought out the worst in people.

Windows were smashed. Glass and fresh blood gleamed in the sunlight. Men and women fought in the streets for impractical items. A fifty-inch TV wouldn't save them from the epidemic. Liquor wouldn't fend off the attacks. Jewelry wouldn't keep their loved ones safe. They were stupid and materialistic, and they were going to die. Instead of running or securing themselves in a locked building, they were out here stealing. Katie dodged past two men carrying a sofa out of a broken storefront window. Another man ran at her and tried to grab her bag. She swung around and drove a kick into his chest. He sprawled backward looking shocked and then scrambled away. No one and nothing was going to keep her away from her little sister, not this time. Katie looked up to see the soldier looking at her surprised and slightly amused. "What?" She asked defensively.

"No, nothing. Just surprised you landed that kick is all." He said with a smirk. "Impressive. I'm Eric by the way."

"Mia."

"Katie."

"Where are you guys headed?" Eric kept checking their perimeter. "Do you know anywhere we can ride this out?"

"We're going to my parents' place over on Oak Hill Avenue. My little sister Kacey is home alone right now, and she needs me." Katie hoisted her bag higher on her shoulders and started winding her way through the bodies and the looters. Glass crunched under her sneakers.

Eric let Mia follow after her friend while he took up the rear, "My unit was called in after the police were unable to contain the situation. We were supposed to take the targets into custody. If that failed, the next order was shoot to kill. I never actually thought I would be put in that situation, though." Eric paused for a moment, lost in thought. He had only signed up for the Guard to help pay for his college. In the back of his mind, he always knew it was a possibility that he would see combat, but he never thought it would actually happen. Eric's face hardened as he thought about the decisions he made that had led up to this moment. "You live your life. You go out drinking, and you ignore the people you care about because you're too tired or too drunk to deal with their shit, you know? Then something happens that makes you take a good hard look at yourself." Eric's voice filled with self-loathing, "You know the last thing I said to my mom? I told her I was too busy hanging out with my buds, and I would call her back later. Now I'll probably never get to talk to her again. Not the real her anyway."

Katie glanced over her shoulder at him and saw his name patch. "Lee? Your last name's Lee?" She stopped walking. "Was your mom the nurse?"

Eric nodded. His mouth was a taut, thin line. His Adam's apple quivered, "Every time I close my eyes I see that news footage of her getting bitten. She wasn't even supposed to be there. She took an extra shift to cover for her coworker who wanted to go to her kid's little league game."

"My mom was a trial patient," Mia said quietly. The two of them looked at one another sharing a palpable loss that made Katie's heartache.

"We need to keep moving," Katie said as a woman on the ground started twitching. "We may not have much time."

The three of them watched as their town descended into madness. It was insane to imagine that all of these bodies were your everyday grocers, baristas, and soccer moms. "How could three people cause this much damage?" Katie asked as they passed a minivan that had crashed into a stoplight. The light was flashing red.

"They didn't." Eric was looking straight ahead. His left foot was pointing forward, and his right foot was a pace behind. He slowly lowered his gun from its upright position and aimed it at something moving on the other side of an overturned truck.

Katie backed up slowly until she was standing beside Eric. "What do we do?" She whispered while keeping her eyes on the figure that was still only partially visible.

"See the alley to your left?" Eric's voice was barely audible as he pushed his gun's safety into the off position. There was a light click as it slid into place.

"Yeah." Katie glanced towards the alleyway. Mia was still a few paces in front of them. She was shaking.

"You and Mia go that way. I'll meet you between Spruce and Sycamore Street." Eric had the gun pressed against his shoulder. His finger rested against the outside of the trigger.

Katie placed her hand lightly on Mia's arm. Mia jumped at her touch, and when she turned around silent tears trickled down her face. Katie took Mia's hand and tried to lead her down the deserted alleyway, but she wouldn't move. She just looked back towards the truck.

That's when Katie saw the person move out from behind the bed of the vehicle. She recognized the slender build, even without the dark hair.

"Mom?" Mia's voice broke and she took a step forward. Her knife clattered to the ground. Her mom's head tilted to one side and then slowly rotated to the other. "Mom!" Mia's voice was pained and breathy. She struggled against Katie's restraining hand.

"Mia, no!" Katie grabbed onto Mia's wrist with both hands and dug in her heels.

Mia's mom pulled her lips back to bare her teeth. Dried blood stained her mouth. Her hospital armband glinted in the sun, and her maroon gown fluttered in the breeze.

"Mom...mom, it's me. It's Mia. It's me!" Mia's voice pleaded across the street.

What used to be Mia's mom charged at them. Her bare feet scraped across the pavement with every step. Mia broke free from Katie's grasp and ran towards her mom. Katie fell backward landing on tiny shards of glass that still littered the sidewalk. She watched as her friend raced towards the monster her mother had become.

A single shot rang out across the street. The silence immediately following it was deafening. For a single moment, the chaos around them was completely still. The bullet had gone straight through the skull. Mia's mom staggered in mid stride. She dropped to her knees and then fell, face forward, onto the asphalt.

Mia screamed and dropped to her own knees. She started beating her legs and doubled over letting out the most primal sound Katie had ever heard. Mia began slamming her head into the pavement. The shrill keening escalated in volume as her grief mounted. Katie crawled over to her and pulled her upright. Mia tried to push her away, but Katie held her tight.

"Guys," Eric said, "there's more of them."

His voice brought him to Mia's attention. She elbowed Katie in the chest and scrambled towards him. Her grief doubled her strength. Katie grabbed her ankles, but Mia kicked her off. She got to her feet and rammed her shoulders into Eric's stomach. He staggered backward a few paces before he was able to brace himself against her attack.

"Mia, it wasn't her anymore!" Katie yelled at her. "Stop it! You saw her. That thing wasn't your mom. She had blood on her mouth, Mia. Blood. Those people at the college, the ones who started attacking the students? That is what she had become. She was one of them."

Mia turned from her attack on Eric and looked at Katie. "She was my mom." Mia's eyes were full of sorrow and desperation. She turned to look at her mom's body sprawled in the street. This was the woman who had worked three jobs to help pay for her college, the woman who had put off her chemo treatments because she thought showing up bald at a high school graduation would embarrass her daughter, the woman who had sacrificed so much for her. She didn't deserve this, to be gunned down in the middle of the street because some scientists in a lab created a horrible new drug. This wasn't fair. She had given so much of herself, and now she was just lying there. She looked so frail and helpless. Mia walked towards her mother. She didn't deserve this. That single thought consumed every part of Mia. She didn't deserve this.

There were four more patients emerging from behind vehicles. They were joined by several pedestrians that all had bloodstained clothing and irregular gashes along their arms and upper body. Eric grabbed Katie around the waist and threw her over his shoulder. He headed for the alleyway away from the approaching Recusant patients and their new victims.

"We can't just leave her!" Katie yelled at him.

"She won't come with us willingly, and right now she's more of a liability."

"But she's going to die!"

"And if we stay and try to drag her with us, so will we!" Eric started jogging towards the end of the alley.

From her position over his shoulder, Katie could see Mia kneeling by her mother. She had pulled her mom's head into her lap and was stroking her cheek. They made it around the corner of the building before Mia's screams started. Katie grabbed two fistfuls of the back of Eric's shirt and closed her eyes. After they had gone a few blocks and the screams had faded, Eric set Katie back on her feet. He leaned his gun against the nearest building. He took her face in his hands and rested his forehead on hers. "Look at me." He said. His blue eyes stared into hers. "You can grieve later. I need you to be strong right now. Do what you gotta do, ok?"

Katie stared back at him. She was having trouble breathing.

"Katie, stay with me, ok? Think about your sister. What was your sister's name? Kerry?"

"Kacey."

"Alright, you have to focus for Kacey, ok? Can you do that?" He absent-mindedly stroked her cheek with his thumb and then caught himself.

"Yeah. Yeah, I can do that." Katie steeled herself. She had to think about Kacey. She could deal with everything later. She closed her eyes and took in a deep breath. She could do this. Her eyes flew open. "Where's my knife?" She looked around and then back the way they had come. "I must have dropped it while I was trying to stop—," She couldn't say Mia's name. If she said it, it would be admitting Mia was dead, and she couldn't do that yet.

"Here." Eric pulled a knife out of his combat boot and handed it to her. "Use mine."

"Thanks." The knife was heavier than it looked. The hilt was black and ribbed to fit a man's natural grip. The steel was heavily polished and blinded her momentarily as it caught the sunlight. Katie adjusted her ball cap. "Ahh!" She winced and pulled her hand away. Tiny shards of glass were embedded in her palms from when she fell.

"Let me see." Eric took her hand in his and looked over the area. "We're going to need to get that taken care of. Got any first aid kit stuff at your parents' place?"

"Yeah. We were always clumsy growing up. Mom made sure to keep stuff on hand." For the first time, Katie wondered if her own mother was ok. She's out of town. She'll be fine. Think about Kacey. "We need to get moving." She pulled her hand away from his.

"You said Oak Hill Avenue, right?"

"Yeah. It's just a few streets over, now." Katie repositioned her bag again and started walking in the direction of her childhood home. This neighborhood hadn't been as ransacked as the rest of town. It was almost eerie how untouched everything looked. Cars lined the streets. It looked like at any moment someone would walk out of their house and check the mail or get in their car to go pick up their kids from soccer practice. Eric kept scanning the area. Wind chimes rattled in the breeze. The notes sang out over the deserted streets. Katie walked closer to Eric. He looked at her and smirked.

"What's that?" Katie leaned her head to the right to get a better look at the vehicles that were parked along the street. At the end of the row, there was a group of people with ripped clothing shoving one another. They were tugging on the door handles of a white car. Some of them were beating their palms against the windows leaving bloody handprints behind. Between the rows of shoulders, Katie saw something move inside the car. "There's someone in there." Her eyes grew wide.

Eric looked at the crowd milling around, "There have to be at least ten of them."

"Right. You coming?" Katie tightened her grip on the knife he had loaned her.

"You're insane." Eric looked at her with disbelief and slight admiration. "You got any combat training?"

"I took karate when I was like eight, and my dad taught my sister and me how to shoot when we were growing up."

"So not really. Ok, look, you know those zombie movies where people always say to go for the head? Well, this time, they seem to be right. The brain is affected. If you take out the brain, you take out the threat. Make sense?"

"Zombies. You know, I always thought that if this ever happened in real life I would be better prepared. I'd just grab my zombie survival kit and hole up at Sam's Club. But now here I am, staring at a horde of zombies, about to run in like a crazy person with a knife." Katie turned her head to look at him, "I'm the person I yell at in horror movies."

Eric chuckled, "Or we could go with option B. Your dad taught you how to shoot? You remember well enough?" Katie nodded while he spoke. "You take the gun and cover me. I'll take the knife. All you have to do is not shoot me. Think you can do that?"

"Yeah." The gun felt awkward in her grasp as he took the knife and handed her the rifle.

"You got this. It'll be a piece of cake." He smiled lopsidedly and winked at her. Once his back was to her his bravery melted away. It was all he could do to make his legs move toward the crowd.

As Eric got closer, he could see a small girl in the back seat of the white car. She was frantically trying to stay as far away from all of the windows and doors as she could. Seeing the girl made Eric tap into his last reserves of courage. He took a deep breath and breathed out slowly. He squared his shoulders and readied his knife. He ran to the closest zombie and rammed his knife into the guy's temple. The blade sunk in up to the hilt. He jerked the knife out and drove it into the eye socket of the next one. Behind him, Katie fired the rifle. Her first bullet ricocheted off of the car's left fender. She cussed under her breath and adjusted her aim. Shoot on the exhale. She could hear her father's voice in her head. She fired another round into the shoulder of one of the zombies that were now focused on Eric. Just a little higher. Her third shot went completely through its head. The bullet had enough momentum that it traveled into the skull of the zombie behind the one she had been aiming at. Both of them immediately dropped to the ground. Katie kept firing, and two more zombies fell to the pavement. Eric stabbed and twisted the knife through the back of a woman's head. He placed his foot on the small of her back and kicked her away from him, freeing his weapon. The force of her impact knocked down another zombie. Eric lifted the knife, clutched it in both hands, and plunged it down into the fallen zombie's skull. His lunge brought him down to one knee.

There were only two left. One charged at Eric and tackled him. Eric lost his grip on the hilt of the knife and rolled onto his back, trying to keep the zombie at arm's length. Katie aimed and pulled the trigger. The gun responded with a light clicking sound. She was out of ammo. While Eric was struggling with one of the zombies, the other one was headed towards her. Blood was smeared across its cheek. It looked at her hungrily and smiled gruesomely as it approached. Katie grabbed the gun by the barrel. The metal seared her skin and the heat made her palms itch. She could see Eric fighting to keep a good handle on the zombie that was on top of him as it writhed in his grasp. Spit drooled out of the zombie's mouth and strung down towards Eric's face. As the second one got closer to her, Katie ran forward to meet it and swung the butt of the gun like a bat into its head. The zombie stumbled. Katie kicked him in the gut knocking him to the ground. She placed her foot on his chest and drove the butt of the gun into his skull with all of her strength until bits of brain matter splattered onto the hem of her pants and across the asphalt.

Katie looked up to see the zombie on top of Eric chomping at the air. His teeth were barely missing Eric's cheek. Katie raced over to them and slammed the butt of the gun into the side of the zombie's head. Eric pushed him off and grabbed the knife that was sticking out of the female zombie's skull. He stabbed the last zombie six times before he allowed himself to begin to breathe again. He looked up at Katie who was standing over him. She was shaking.

Eric stood up slowly and wrapped one arm around her. He pulled her into his chest and she let relief wash over her. Out of the corner of her eye she, saw the little girl move in the car. Katie pulled away from Eric and walked over to the blood smeared vehicle. The little girl looked uncertain.

"It's ok. You can come out now." Katie reassured her.

The girl unlocked the door and pushed it open. She stepped out of the car and looked at all of the dead bodies around her.

"Where are you, parents?" Katie squatted down to look the little girl in the eye. The girl looked towards the bushes on the other side of the car. Katie could see an arm sprawled on the lawn. She took the little girl's hand, "You're going to come with us, ok? We'll keep you safe." The little girl nodded.

"What's your name?" Eric asked.

The girl ducked behind Katie. "Gracie," she said timidly. She held onto Katie's pinkie and ring finger.

"I'm Katie, and this is Eric." Katie stood up, "Let's go this way, ok?" The girl nodded as Katie led her away from the massacre. Katie slung the gun over her shoulder as they walked. They heard the rhythmic whirling of helicopters in the distance, but they couldn't see them yet.

"That's it." Katie pointed at a light blue house in the distance. There weren't any lights on. Katie had a sickening feeling in the pit of her stomach. As they got closer, they could see blood smeared across the siding. Katie let go of Gracie's hand. She ran up the worn, creaking porch steps and pounded on the door. "Kace?" She yelled for her sister as she pressed her nose to the window pane. "Kacey?"

Something moved in the shadows of the hallway to the living room. Katie's heart caught in her throat. She backed away as the lock clicked. The door eased open and Kacey looked through the gap at her sister. Katie jerked the door open and grabbed her little sister in a bear hug. She kissed the top of her head and squeezed her tighter while she wiped the tears out of her eyes.

"Come on, we need to get inside." Katie held the door while the others walked into the house.

Eric started pushing the couch up against the closed door once they were all inside. Katie put her back against the arm of the sofa and pushed with her feet until it slid into place as a makeshift barricade. Kacey went into the kitchen, and they could hear the screech of wood on the tile as she shoved the dining room table against the back door.

"Have you heard from mom or dad?" Katie asked her sister while Eric peered out of the blinds into the street.

"Mom called earlier. She said there are roadblocks around the city, and they aren't letting anyone in or out. I still haven't heard from dad."

Katie walked over to the hall closet and shuffled around the extra toilet paper and the q-tips until she found the first aid kit.

"Here, let me do that." Eric took the plastic box from her, and they went to the kitchen sink. Kacey and Gracie sat on the living room floor and turned on the news. From the kitchen, Eric and Katie could hear the news anchors telling people to stay in their homes. Eric turned on the faucet and let the water run over the tips of his fingers while the temperature adjusted. Once the water was cold, he took Katie's hands and guided them under the stream. She winced a little as the water ran over the tiny shards of embedded glass and the shredded, seared skin that was already beginning to pucker. The cool water offered some relief. Eric pulled the glass out of her palms with a pair of tweezers and then applied antiseptic. While he was wrapping her hands in bandages, Gracie came into the kitchen.

"My mommy always said kisses will make you heal faster." She swayed back and forth from her heels to the balls of her feet while she talked.

Eric smirked and looked at Katie. He took her hands and gently brought them to his lips. He maintained eye contact with Katie as he kissed each of her hands. "I think your mommy was right," Eric said to Gracie while he smiled at Katie. Katie blushed and smiled back at him.

"Let's go back in the living room," Katie shook her head and rolled her eyes at Eric. She put her bandaged hand on Gracie's shoulder and guided her back into the living area.

The mantle was covered in Marine Corps memorabilia, tiny porcelain frogs that Katie's mom had been collecting for years, and a few family photos. Kacey was still sitting on the tan carpet on the floor. Gracie snuggled up next to Kacey and put her head in the other girl's lap. Kacey absent-mindedly stroked Gracie's hair.

Katie and Eric sat down beside the other two. The station was showing footage from a news helicopter as it flew over the town. From the air, you could see the piles of bodies that lined the streets and some of the zombies milling around aimlessly. The video footage shrank into the right-hand corner of the screen as the news anchor came back on.

"The government has taken swift action to contain the situation. Everyone is to remain indoors until the affected citizens can be taken into custody. The CDC would like us to remind you that this epidemic does seem to be contagious. If you are exposed to any bodily fluids of an infected person, please separate yourself from friends and loved ones until you can be reached by officials." A S.W.A.T. team had entered the field of vision on the live footage while the reporter spoke. They meticulously cleared each building. A few team members entered each of the premises. Sometimes they came out with civilians. Sometimes they came out alone. A military man joined the news anchor. His chest was laden with medals that glinted under the florescent lighting. Katie never heard what he was saying because someone pounded on the front door. The knocking drowned out the broadcast.

"This is Sergeant Haskell. Is anyone in there?" The man's voice boomed with authority.

"Yes," Katie yelled as she scampered towards the door, "there are four of us!"

"Anyone bit?"

"No, Sir."

"Alright, open the door slowly, and everyone keep your arms in the air."

Katie and Eric pushed the couch out of the way. Eric unbolted the door and slowly turned the knob. The door creaked open.

"Gracie, honey, put your hands up like this, ok?" Katie said as she raised her hands.

Some members of the S.W.A.T. team entered the house cautiously and started checking the other rooms. Team members started patting Katie, Eric, Kacey, and Gracie down.

"Any weapons?"

"There's a knife and an empty rifle in the kitchen." Eric jerked his head towards the other room. The sergeant motioned for two of his men to check it out.

The soldiers who had been looking through the rooms came back. "All clear."

"Alright, let's move these civilians to the med tents and keep moving." Haskell walked out of the door followed by most of his men.

"This way." One of the soldiers pointed his rifle towards the part of town that had already been cleared.

The men escorting them formed a ring around the four of them as they made their way to the edge of town. They approached a yellow hazmat tent. The soldiers watched them enter the tent and then headed back out to rejoin their team.

"Strip, please." A lady covered in a hazmat suit pulled a thin curtain closed between Eric and the girls. She examined each of the girls, methodically checking them for any lacerations. "What happened to your hands?" The lady looked suspiciously at Katie and gestured to someone at the mouth of the tent.

"I fell on some glass, and I burnt myself." Katie grimaced as the woman undid her bandages to get a closer look.

"I'd like to keep you for observation," the woman backed away from Katie, "just to make sure you didn't get any infected fluids in your cuts." A guard came around the edge of the curtain. "You two can put on the green scrubs over there." The lady gestured to a pile of clothes. "You," she looked at Katie, "need to put on the orange ones. Officer Clifton will show you to an observation tent."

"How...how long are you going to watch her?" Kacey was pale and panicked as she slid the green top over her head. She tugged her hair out of the collar and jerked the bottom of her shirt into place.

"The symptoms should be visible in a few hours if she's been infected. If she's still fine by then, she can find you outside of the quarantine."

"And if she's not?" Kacey's voice rose. The woman didn't say anything, she just looked away. Officer Clifton grabbed Katie's upper arm and started leading her away. Kacey clutched at the officer as he tried to escort Katie out of the tent.

"A little help in here?" The woman called out. Eric pushed aside the curtain as another officer came in to subdue Kacey.

"Watch over them, ok?" Katie said over her shoulder. Eric nodded. His breath quickened, but he tried to remain calm on the outside. He adjusted the green scrubs they had given him and took the two girls outside of the tent to where the red cross was handing out food and water to the townspeople who had been cleared.

Katie was taken to another tent with clear dividers and stretchers. The orange scrubs made her feel like a prisoner.

"Lie down, please." Officer Clifton gestured to the closest stretcher.

"Katie?" The man on the other side of the plastic sheet craned his neck to see her.

"Dad!" Katie smiled at him while the officer strapped her to the cold, metal stretcher. The tent smelled like antiseptic. Her dad was covered in a sheen of sweat. "Dad?"

"Too late for me, Katiebug." He smiled, but his eyes were full of sadness. "Where's your sister, your mom, are they..."

"They're fine. Mom was out of town when it happened, and Kacey was already cleared to go in the first tent."

"Baby girl, if you make it out of here, I—," his body seized up as he tried to speak, "I need you to tell your mom and sister that I love them, ok?" His neck tensed up. His breathing was labored. "Tell them I should have been there for more little league games," Katie's dad groaned in pain as he struggled to get the words out, "and parent-teacher conferences."

"Dad they know how—"

"Katie let me finish. I don't have long." The blood drained from his face. "Tell them I'm sorry, ok? I need you to be strong for them when this is over." His eyes started to dart back and forth, unable to focus. "They're going to need you." He convulsed at the end of his sentence.

"Dad?" Katie fought against her restraints. Her legs and arms struggled to find any give in the straps that had her pinned to the stretcher.

"I need a sedative in here!" Officer Clifton yelled to a nurse.

"I love you, Katie" Her dad looked at her as he tried to keep himself from shaking.

"Dad? Dad!" Katie yelled as nurses surrounded her. She moved her head trying to see her father. She felt a needle slide into her arm. "I love you!" She shouted as her mind became hazy. Her eyes closed even though she fought to keep them open. The sedative took hold of her, and the world went black.

After a few hours, Katie came back to consciousness. She blinked and squinted as a nurse shined a tiny flashlight in her pupils. "Do you know your name?"

"It's Katie." Katie pulled her head away from the nurse.

"Good news, Katie. You appear to have no symptoms of the infection. I'm going to take off your restraints, ok? Just lie still."

"What happened to my dad?" Katie turned her head to look at the empty stretcher behind the plastic.

"He was contaminated. We gave him an injection to help him along peacefully." The nurse touched Katie's arm. "He didn't suffer."

Katie tried to fight back the tears as the nurse removed her restraints.

"Please change into these." The nurse handed Katie a pair of green scrubs as she sat up.

Katie felt numb as she changed her clothes. An officer came and showed her the way out of the observation tent. Katie followed, not really paying attention. It was close to twilight now.

"Katie!" Kacey ran to her sister and hugged her. Her mother followed closely behind and put her arms around both of her daughters.

Katie pulled away and looked at them. "Dad...dad didn't make it." Hot tears ran down her face as the words came out of her mouth. Her mother sat down on the ground and placed her head in her hands. Kacey knelt down beside her mom and cried on her shoulder. Katie's shoulders started to heave as she fought the sobs that were trying to finally escape. Behind her, she felt a strong chest against her back. Katie turned around and buried her face into Eric's chest as his arms encircled her. This was the safest she had felt all day. She let her grief wash over her in waves. She thought about Mia and her dad and all of the devastation she had witnessed.

"Where's Gracie?" Katie mumbled into Eric's shirt.

"She found her aunt. She's with her family now." Eric held Katie tighter as she nodded.

"Here, take one and pass it on." A lady handed them a box of candles with a lighter.

Eric and Katie each took a candle. Katie handed the box to her mom. The survivors all stood in silence, mourning their loved ones. Bodies of the infected were being burned in the streets of the town. They could smell the smoke from outside of the quarantine. The flames of their candles flickered and shone out in the dark as the flames from the burning bodies roared in a crackling cackle. The living and the dead were joined, for one last time, in a vigil of flame.

END

DEADVILLE

by Tessa Leon

Chapter One

"For today's homework you are to write a 5000 word essay on the female philosopher Hypatia," said Professor Singh to his class of 60, in the large college auditorium.

"Yawn! Is he done yet?" asked Sonya.

"Sssh!" responded Helen. "I need to write this down."

When the class was dismissed, the philosophy students headed outside to the courtyard. It was last class of the day, so everyone hung out, firming up Friday night's plans.

Helen's classmates and best friends hung out near the fountain.

"Is everyone going to the party at Epsilon tonight?" asked Jane.

Mariko and Sonya both responded with resounding yeses. They looked at Helen.

"Nope, not me. I'm room-bound tonight."

"Again?" asked Sonya in her Finnish accent. "You missed last weekend's party too."

"Last weekend was great! I met Juan at the party!" said Mariko in her heavy Japanese accent.

"I haven't met anyone yet, but there's hope right?" said Jane. "Perhaps I should borrow some makeup from Sonya." She pulled out a mirror and had a look at her plain face.

"You look fine Jane," said Helen. "I just need to get this essay done. I have to work at the coffee shop all weekend, and I still need to do my math and my astronomy homework too."

The women all groaned.

"How long is this going to go on?" asked Sonya.

"As long as I need the cash," said Helen. "You guys go and have fun! Tell me all about the party when you get back home tonight. Or, tomorrow morning, ha ha!" She waved them off.

The three ladies headed off to get ready for the party, while Jane headed for her own dorm room. She left the door open and sat at her desk.

She had just started doing some research on her laptop when her friends poked their heads into her room.

"Last chance for fun!" said Mariko.

"Nope, you guys go and have tons of fun! And be careful!" said Helen. "Remember there was that student who went missing last week."

"Party pooper!" said Sonya.

"Bye!" said Jane, with her half-hearted attempt at makeup.

Helen breathed a sigh of relief. Now she could get some work done. Should she close the door? She peered up and down the hallway, but it was quiet. Likely everyone had gone out for dinner, or was already at a party. She'd tackle dinner later. Right now she wanted to outline her essay on Hypatia, Alexandrian philosopher, who'd been brutally murdered by Christians. And to think that they bashed Muslims nowadays. She shook her head.

The Epsilon building was located right next to her dorm. Unfortunately, she could already hear pounding music, so she closed her window.

It wasn't so great being stuck in her room all night. She took a break to eat some leftover pizza from her mini fridge, but then it was back to work. Having to work to pay for college was frustrating at times. Her parents helped, but it simply wasn't enough.

She had just finished her essay, and was going to get started on her math homework, when she heard a piercing scream fill the air.

Chapter Two

Sonya, Jane, and Mariko were squished into the corner of Epsilon's living room. The room was packed with people, with a loud pop song overwhelming most of the conversation.

"I can't hear what you're saying," yelled Mariko.

"Great party!" yelled Sonya back at her.

"Hey, some guy gave me a bunch of lollipops," said Jane.

Mariko pointed at them. "If you suck on that, you'll get high," she said.

"Yep, it's never just candy at a party," said Sonya.

"Oh, but it was safe last weekend," said Jane. "It only gave a nice light buzz. I was completely within my faculties."

"You can say that again. I hadn't realized you were high," said Sonya.

Jane handed them out to everyone. "Here you go. We'll watch out for one another anyway."

"I wonder where Juan is?" asked Mariko. "He said he'd be here."

"It's still early. I'm sure he's on his way," said Sonya.

"Ooh! I hope I'm at the right party! There might be something else happening tonight. I'd better text him," said Mariko, as the song finally died down.

Jane took the wrapper off her lollipop and stuck it in her mouth. Sonya did the same. Mariko was busy with her phone.

"What on earth is that shrieking?"

"I don't know," said Sonya. She pulled the drapes aside and looked out the window. The others at the party were oblivious to anything happening outside. A new CD started playing and drowned out any other sounds.

***

Helen was just heading to the window to see who was shrieking, when a red splat struck it, and its ooze dripped slowly down. She backed off.

"Ahhhh," screamed a voice outside.

Helen peered out the window.

"What on earth?" she asked, her eyes deceiving her. Outside her window Juan, or what had been Juan was reaching up at her window. He had a huge hole in his head, like someone had shot him, but still, he kept on moving. His jaw was spasmodically making chewing movements on what appeared to be a severed hand.

"Oh my god. How I am going to tell Mariko?"

She watched as Professor Singh ran up to Juan and shot him in the head. Finally, his body dropped to the ground.

"How odd," said Helen. "It was almost like he was a zombie."

"Lock your doors and windows," yelled Professor Singh. "Pull the drapes! There are zombies out here!"

Helen waved at him and did as he said. She rushed over and closed her door and locked it. She grabbed her phone and dialed 911. For some reason, it rang busy. She decided to call campus security instead.

"Hello, security? There is some sort of disturbance happening in the courtyard. Oh, you already know? Yes, I'll stay in my room, thanks."

Helen hung up. She didn't know what exactly was happening outside, but she'd better stay safely in here. Perhaps it was another riot, like the one they had in '97.

She just noticed that someone was in her bathroom. They must have snuck in when she had her door open.

Chapter Three

The party was rapidly turning into a drug party. People were becoming more outgoing and social. The noise level of the party had just cranked up a notch, with conversations competing with the fast pop music.

Mariko had given up on trying to track down Juan. She was chatting with guys, while licking her lollipop. Sonya and Jane has long since discarded theirs, and were pouring themselves drinks from the punch bowl. They'd long since forgotten about the noise from outside, attributing it to a drunk college frat boy.

"Oh look," said Jane. "There's that nasty Bev, over there in the corner."

"Ugh, can't stand her!" said Mariko, giving up her chat with the guys.

"That girl is a bully. Even when she pretends to be nice she has an ulterior motive," said Sonya.

"No lollipops for her!" said Jane, and everyone laughed with her.

"Seriously though, she could use one. Look at how uptight she looks over there. Everyone is avoiding her."

"I can't stand people like that," said Jane. "Remember she kept on asking me why I was going to the bathroom during math class? None of her frickin' business."

"Not one social attribute in that one," said Sonya, taking a sip of her drink.

"Come on guys, I didn't come here to talk about Bev," said Mariko. "I'm here to have fun!"

"I don't know about you, but I'm famished! Let's see what's on the buffet table," said Sonya, leading them away from the drinks table and towards the food.

"Now that you mention it, I do have the munchies," said Jane. "Hey look, a deli tray!"

"Check it out, meatballs!" said Sonya.

"Yuck, I hope they have some veggie food here," said Mariko eyeing the table. She found the veggie platter and filled up her plate.

"Hey, I feel a bit nauseous. I don't think that lollipop and the vodka got along. I'm going to the bathroom," said Jane.

"I'll check on you if you're not back in five minutes," said Mariko.

Jane left to use the bathroom out in the hallway.

"No sign of Juan?" asked Sonya.

Mariko shook her head.

"It's okay, we'll meet up later. I'm not his mommy, he can do what he likes," she replied.

"Well, who needs to be saddled down at a party!" said Sonya.

The music was dying down. Again, they heard sounds coming from outside. They headed to the window and pulled open the drapes.

"Cool!" said a voice from behind them.

What appeared to be the figure of student was madly racing around the courtyard. Except it was lit up with fire.

"Holy crap, what's going on out there?" asked Sonya.

"Why doesn't he drop and roll?" asked Mariko.

Surrounding the burning man were several people wielding various types of weapons. The burning man's arms reached out to grab one of them. His jaws were frantically moving, appearing as though he were trying to bite one of them.

The girls heard cries of "zombie!" coming from outside.

"Wow, entertainment!" said a voice from behind them.

Chapter Four

Helen walked towards the bathroom.

"Excuse me? This is a private room. The public washroom is down the hallway," she said to her private visitor.

The girl in the bathroom seemed to just be standing in front of the mirror, looking at her face. She didn't say anything.

Helen decided she had to start getting tough. Students couldn't just barge into her room at any time they wanted. There was a code of entry in the dormers.

Helen walked into her bathroom. She tapped the girl on the shoulder.

"Hello! This is my bathroom," she said.

The girl turned to face her. One of her eyes was missing. Her lips were gone and much of her face was bloodied, like she had been in an accident. There was a terrible stench of decay mixed with the metallic smell of blood. If there were any doubt that she was wearing stage makeup, it was gone when a maggot slipped out of her eye socket.

"Eek!" cried Helen.

The girl turned completely around and started walking towards Helen. She raised her hands up.

"Get away from me you freak!" cried Helen.

***

In the guy's dormer room Jane was using the private handicapped washroom, as there was no ladies' room here. She vomited into the toilet, and felt better. Perhaps she shouldn't mix drugs and alcohol. She rinsed her mouth out and washed her face off.

By now her efforts to cover her face with makeup were gone. But she felt so awful that she didn't care by this point.

Her shoulder was really itchy so she reached inside her blouse to scratch. When she pulled her hand away, it was bloody. Horrified, she pushed her blouse aside. A large flap of skin was hanging down.

She screamed. Was this part of the drug's side effects? To hallucinate? She didn't know what else to do but hunt through the medicine cabinet. She found a first aid kit and cleaned the wound. She sprayed on antiseptic, and then carefully pushed the skin back up. She placed a large bandage on it.

She didn't see anything else wrong, so she decided to head back to the party and tell her friends she was calling it a night.

***

"Holy shit, what is happening?" asked Sonya.

Outside, there were a pack of professors brandishing weapons. Could it be that they were fighting off a pack of zombies? The man on fire was still running around trying to attack people.

The president of Epsilon had turned off the music, and was yelling out instructions.

"Hello everyone! The Faculty wants to inform us that the campus is under zombie attack! This is not a joke! Everyone is requested to return to their dorm rooms ASAP and do not engage with anyone. Thank you for coming to our party. Goodnight."

He then started guiding people out the door.

Sonya and Mariko decided they'd better wait for Jane to come back from the bathroom. They tensed as they saw Bev heading towards them.

"Why do you girls always hang out together?" asked Bev. She was short and had fake blonde hair. She was standing there holding her beer and smirking from behind her Chanel eyeglasses.

"Because we have friends, Bev," Sonya said to her.

"Oh, I have friends too. They invited me to the Vanderbilt party last week, at their big mansion down the street."

"Well, that's awesome," said Mariko, trying not to roll her eyes. "Shouldn't we try to find out what is happening outside?"

"Really?" said Bev. "Because you seem a bit sarcastic to me."

"You started it," said Sonya. "You really need to be more respectful towards people."

"Hey bitch!" started Bev.

"Oh look, Jane's back!" said Mariko. "I think it's time we headed to Juan's party," she suggested.

***

Chapter Five

"Get away from me," cried Helen. The zombie thing came at her.

Helen looked madly around the room for a weapon. What would be in a dorm room that she could use as a weapon? She looked madly around. Books. Pens. Bar fridge. Knapsack. Baseball bat.

That's it, she could use her roommate's baseball bat. The zombie was trying to grab at her arms. Helen picked up the baseball bat and whacked it over the head.

The zombie's head exploded, brains and blood everywhere.

"Ugh," said Helen. "Sarah, is that you?"

She peered more closely at the zombie, and realized that it had been her roommate, who was supposed to be out for the night.

She started crying, but then tried to pull herself together. From what she knew of horror films, the gore on her face could be dangerous. She dropped the bat and rushed to the bathroom to wash up.

Inside the bathroom she stripped off her clothes and headed to the shower. She spent a good twenty minutes ensuring that not a speck of zombie blood remained on her skin. She turned off the water, then used a towel to dry off. Wrapping it around her she carefully picked her clothes off the ground and dropped them in the bin. She then fished bleach, gloves, and a cloth from under the sink, and scrubbed down the floor, as well as the sink and mirror. There was no telling what Sarah had touched as she was turning into a zombie.

She then got dressed. She grabbed her knapsack and carefully opened the door to the hallway. Ten zombies loomed outside. They curiously peered at her as she widened the door. Nope, there was no way she was getting out that way.

As the zombies reached towards her, she hastily shut the door. She was stuck in here, with a dead zombie. Helen grimaced at the mutilated body lying on the ground.

Chapter Six

Jane finished up in the bathroom. She was starting to feel better. In fact, she was downright hungry. She decided to head back to the party, but most likely she would have to call it quits and head to bed.

As she walked backed into Epsilon's living room, she saw Bev hovering over the group. What did she want?

Jane couldn't stand Bev. Bev had taunted her in philosophy class for weeks, until Professor Singh had put an end to it, threatening to call her out for bullying. It was prohibited on campus. Still, it did not stop her from putting in a jab every now and then.

Soon Jane grew to pity Bev, who obviously dealt with bullying from her parents on an ongoing basis. But tonight, enough was enough. Jane was hungry.

Sonya and Mariko waved frantically at her. They watched as Jane strode up and bit Bev in the shoulder.

"Ahh!' screamed Bev. "What the!"

"Oh my god," cried Mariko. "What have you done?"

Jane lifted up her head and licked her lips. "Wow, I don't know what got into me!" she said.

"I'm going to have you arrested for assault!" said Bev, holding her sore shoulder. There was a small amount of blood, but not any more than normal with an animal bite.

"Let's get out of here!" said Sonya. She grabbed her friends' hands and they left the end of the party.

As they hurried out of the building, they saw chaos in the courtyard.

"Damn! What are we going to do?" asked Mariko. "It's a bloodbath out here."

Strangely, as zombies attacked the remaining professors, they avoided their group. They watched as Professor Singh shot a zombie through the head. The zombie went down.

"I think the professor has things under control," said Mariko.

"This way guys," said Jane, and led them around the side of the building. Soon they were safely back in the women's dormitory.

"What's happening?" asked Mariko.

"I think it's the zombie apocalypse," said Sonya.

"Whoa, I thought zombies were only characters in a movie," Mariko replied.

"And what was that biting about?" Sonya asked Jane.

"I don't know what came over me," said Jane. "Am I a zombie?"

Her two friends looked worriedly at her.

"Your eyes seem normal, not like the crazy zombies outside."

"I think I was just angry at Bev, for all this time," said Jane.

"Let's get back to our rooms," said Sonya.

"Let's check on Helen, first," suggested Mariko. She led the way.

***

Inside her room, Helen had tidied up. She'd managed to shove Sarah's zombie body out the window. She'd spent some time mopping up the blood. Fortunately, the flood was linoleum, to making cleaning easier. She'd had to toss out some of her stuffies, but she was an adult anyway, and she had killed a human after all.

Cleaning had calmed her mind somewhat. She was carefully inspecting the floors and walls to be sure that she had left no speck of zombie blood behind. She wrapped up the ends of a large black garbage page, and closed them securely. She could dispose of it once it was safe to leave her room. She still heard moans and groans coming from the hallway, so she was still trapped in her room.

Chapter Seven

Mariko, Sonya, and Jane walked carefully down the hallway. There were some zombies around, but surprisingly, the zombies avoided them. Perhaps zombies only liked older adults? The professors had been fighting them in the courtyard. It was just another mystery of zombie life.

Mariko stopped in front of Helen's door, which was securely shut.

"At least she had the sense to close it," said Sonya.

Mariko knocked on the door. "It's us," she called.

The door slowly opened. Helen's eyes peered out.

"Mariko?" she asked.

"It's just us. It's crazy out there!" said Mariko. "Whoa! It reeks of bleach in here," she said, as Helen opened the door wider to let them into the room. The three women stepped in.

"What's happening out there?" asked Helen. "I had to deal with my zombie roommate! I feel so bad! I had to kill her!"

Mariko and Helen embraced.

"It's not your fault!" said Mariko. "A whole bunch of students have turned into zombies!"

They let go of each other.

"Right guys?" asked Mariko. She turned around.

Sonya was advancing on them. Her eyes glowed a deep red color. Her facial skin was starting to peel away from her face.

"Oh my god! What happened?" cried Mariko.

She and Helen headed to the back of the room. Jane stood near the door looking confused.

"Oh, the bat," said Helen. She looked wildly around the room. Where had she put it during her cleaning?

Sonya raised her arms in the air and advanced towards them.

"Brainnssss," she said. "Must eat brains."

"Is this a joke?" asked Jane, standing there confused.

Helen slipped off to the side to grab the bat. Sonya grabbed onto her wrist.

"Do something!" cried Mariko.

Helen raised the bat and slammed it into Sonya's head. Her head went splat, and her body dropped to the ground.

"Godammit!" cried Helen. "Now I have to clean the friggin' room again!"

"Holy shit! You killed our friend," said Mariko.

"I had to!" yelled Helen. "She was a zombie!"

Mariko started crying. Helen patted her on the shoulder. All this time Jane was cooly watching them from the door.

Helen looked towards Jane.

"Oh no, not you too Jane!"

They watched as Jane's eyes glowed red. Some of her skin was starting to flake off.

"Leave right now Jane! I don't want to have to kill you too!"

"Ohhh I can't watch you kill another of our friends!" said Mariko grimacing.

"I'm not a zombieeeee," said Jane, slurring her words.

"Please leave, while you can," said Helen.

Jane listened and turned away. She left the room. Helen slammed the door after her.

"Holy crap! What just happened?" asked Helen.

Chapter Eight

"We were at a party having fun, when we saw a disturbance outside," began Mariko.

"Yes?" asked Helen. They were both seated on a clean part of her bed, ignoring the gore from Sonya's body around them.

"We saw the professors fighting off zombies in the courtyard. And then they shut down the party. Bev was harassing us, and Jane bit her."

"Jane bit her? And you brought her back here?!" cried Helen.

"Sorry, we didn't know. We just thought she was annoyed." They both looked at each other and started laughing.

After the horrific events of the evening, they both needed a good laugh.

"Well, while you guys were away, I was battling off my zombie roommate."

Mariko looked around the room. "Where is the body?" she asked.

"I pushed it out the window," Helen explained.

"Oh my god. The police are never going to believe this!"

"I know," replied Helen. "We need to do the same with Sonya's body, and then clean up. They'll think they were killed outside."

"Right, let's do it!" said Mariko.

As they were cleaning up, they continued to discuss the evening's events.

"What I don't understand is how the students are suddenly turning into zombies," asked Helen.

"It's strange. Like an infection or something," said Mariko.

"Maybe none of us are immune? We could all turn at any moment," said Helen.

"Very strange. Like there is a common element. It was triggered by something, possibly," her friend replied.

Sonya's brains hadn't made as much of a mess as the last one's. Soon they had the room cleaned up. A second garbage bag now stood by the first.

"We're going to need to dispose of these bags before the police see them in here," said Helen.

"Speaking of which, I haven't heard or seen any around," Mariko said.

"They must have their hands full," said Helen, shrugging.

Mariko was sitting on the bed dead still.

"What's the matter?" Helen asked her.

"I just thought of a common element."

"Yes?" her friend asked.

"When we were at the party they were handing out lollipops," she replied.

"Oh, sugar gets a bad rap, but I doubt it's caused zombiosis."

"No, not that. The lollipops were tainted with some drug, to make us feel happy," said Mariko.

"Didn't we try something like that last weekend? But nothing happened. Why now?"

"I'm not certain," said Mariko. "Oh no!" she cried.

"What's wrong?" asked Helen. "Besides the usual zombies running rampant.

"I had a lollipop too!" Mariko started crying, and put her head down into her hands.

Helen stopped and thought about it.

"If this is a true theory, we'll know for certain when you turn into a zombie!" She grabbed the bat, just in case, but Mariko did not notice. She was too busy crying.

Chapter Nine

Outside Jane was walking around dazed. She saw humans run past her and avoid her. Since she didn't appear to be much of a threat, they left her alone. It had tasted good biting Bev, and she wanted more, but she felt it was wrong to bite humans. Perhaps she could find some deli meat or hot dogs and that would fill her up.

There were several dead bodies, both human, and zombie, in the courtyard. A small gang of professors and campus security were still actively fighting off the more active zombies. Other zombies merely milled around confused, and for the most part were left alone.

Jane briefly wondered if there were different levels of zombies.

***

"Maybe I should leave?" asked Mariko.

"No, please stay. I'm curious as to whether it was the drugs that caused the zombie outbreak. If so, I can get word to the authorities, so at least they can prevent it from happening again."

Helen gripped her bat by her side.

"I wonder what happened to Juan?" asked Mariko. "He never showed at the party."

Helen jumped. "Oh, I'm so sorry."

Mariko raised her head. "Do you know what happened to him?"

"Yes, and it's not good."

Mariko started crying again.

"How did it happen?" she asked.

"I was watching out the window as Juan was trying to get in here. He was a zombie. Professor Singh shot him in the head. I'm so sorry," Helen said, wrapping her arm around Mariko.

"It's okay," Mariko sobbed. "Soon I'll be a zombie too, and you can shoot me in the head."

"No!" said Helen. "We don't know for certain."

***

In the courtyard Jane didn't know what to do with herself. Perhaps she should go back and lock herself in her dorm room? That way she would not be a hindrance to anyone.

"Jane? Is that you?" said a familiar voice. She turned to look at him. Was it her time to die once they realized that she too was a zombie?

***

"Do we just wait here?" asked Mariko.

Helen nodded. "I think it's best. It's safer in here. I've got my bat, I'm armed."

Outside a lot of the noise seemed to be dying down. Helen got up to peer out the window. There were significantly more bodies lying in the courtyard than there had been the last time she looked. So, things were progressing. Until the cavalry arrived there wasn't a lot she could do.

In the distance she thought she saw a woman who looked like Jane. She appeared to be chatting with a guy.

"Say, Mariko, something odd is happening out here," said Helen.

Helen turned to her friend, but she wasn't there. Mariko was at the door trying to move a bookcase in front of it.

"Listen! There's a swarm of zombies out there!"

Mariko was right. Soon there was pounding and banging at the door. The door shook on its frame.

Helen jumped forward to help her friend move the bookcase. She'd take her chances with potentially being stuck in a room with one zombie, rather than the dozen milling outside.

Chapter Ten

Mariko and Helen didn't know what to do. These zombies were smart. They were banging and hammering at the door, trying to get in.

"How do you feel?" Helen asked Mariko.

"Not like a zombie, if that's what you mean," she said.

"Good, so far so good," Helen replied. Though she still clutched the bat in her hands anyway.

The door splintered. The zombies must have been using something to ram it.

"If Jane retained some of her intelligence as a zombie, it stands to reason that these guys have too," said Helen.

"We're going to die," moaned Mariko.

The door splintered inwards, showering splinters and fragments everywhere above the bookcase. The bookcase remained in its place, keeping back the hoard.

Just as suddenly as the door exploded, the zombies were gone.

"Hi guys!" said Jane.

"Jane!" cried Mariko and Helen in unison.

"I've gotten rid of these guys for you now, but I suggest you find a more secure location," Jane said, her words sluggish.

Mariko and Helen hopped over the bookcase and into the hallway.

"This way!" said Jane.

The two women looked hesitantly at each other. Should they trust a zombie? They followed Jane anyway.

Jane led them to Juan's room. Mariko was a bit confused. They walked inside.

"Stay here! I'm helping the professors to round up the zombies outside," said Jane.

She closed the door behind them.

"Oh my god! Juan! You're still alive!" Juan stood by the window. He was indeed well and happy.

Helen was confused. Perhaps she had been mistaken?

"I thought you said he was dead!?" cried Mariko.

Mariko and Juan held each other.

"That was actually my brother!" explained Juan.

Helen looked remorsefully at him.

"I'm so glad your brother was killed and not you!"

Juan let that one go. In fact, Helen had to stifle a giggle. Who could be serious after what everyone had just gone through?

"Oh no! You can't touch me!" said Mariko.

"What?" asked Juan, confused.

"I licked one of the contaminated lollipops. I'm going to turn into a zombie too!"

"Surely it would have happened by now?" reasoned Helen.

"Oh those damn lollipops. You're right, they were what caused the zombiosis." Juan looked concerned. He looked over Mariko's arms, and face, but so far they were clear.

"Tell me Mariko, did you eat a red lollipop, or a green one?"

"What? What difference does that make?"

"Because Professor Singh told me it was the green lollipops that were infected with the zombie drug, not the red ones."

Helen and Juan looked expectantly at her.

"It was... green!" she said.

They all had horrified looks on their faces.

"Ha ha! Fooled you! It was red."

They all burst out laughing.

Someone pounded on the door.

"Yes?" Juan called out.

"Coast is clear," called Jane.

He opened the door. Professor Singh and Jane were standing there.

"It appears campus security has things under control. I recommend you stay here for the night, while we clean up," said Professor Singh. "I'm going to take Jane somewhere safe so we can find a way to cure her, along with some other zombies who helped our cause, rather than killing anyone."

"Bye guys!" called Jane.

"Bye! Take care," her friends called after her.

Juan closed the door. "Who wants pizza?" he asked. "There's always pizza delivery, even during an emergency."

"Me!" cried Helen and Mariko.

"But make mine vegetarian, said Helen and Mariko, at the same time.

"I just had a thought. What happened to Bev?" asked Helen.

Everyone shuddered to think that Bev was now walking around campus as a zombie.

The End.

* 9 7 9 8 2 2 4 7 9 1 6 6 8 *